THE
BLACKBIRD'S
SONG

THE BLACKBIRD'S SONG

Pauline Holdstock

PETER HALBAN
LONDON

FIRST PUBLISHED IN GREAT BRITAIN BY
PETER HALBAN PUBLISHERS LTD
42 South Molton Street
London W1Y 1HB
1990

British Library Cataloguing in Publication Data
Holdstock, Pauline
The blackbird's song.
I. Title
823'.914 [F]

ISBN 1–870015–31–2

Phototypeset by Eastside Typesetters
Printed in Great Britain by WBC Ltd, Bristol

For Emily

Part One

June 1900, Chia-hsien

Martha goes down to wash her feet each time we stop. She clambers over the hot boulders that line the gully until she reaches the muddy stream. She gathers up her torn shift and tucks it round her hips. Then she sits on a low rock and begins to wash the grime and the blood from the taut skin.

I watch. She rinses and laves. She strokes her feet to soothe the hurt. As if they belong to someone else.

I turn away. I turn to William. "She'll soften them more by washing."

"She has to be alone."

But not to pray, William. Not to pray. Sometimes she kneels, right there in the stream. Then she turns her arms in and presses her palms and fingers down on her lean thighs, stretching her long throat so that her head falls back and her face turns full to the loud sun overhead.

No, I have seen her. Not to pray.

William gets up. He wakes James who was sleeping, curled over the bundle, and asks the child to help him with the sling. When it is tied on his back he comes to take Mercy from my breast. She cries but I slip her into the sling.

Martha comes back over the brown rocks. Her feet leave dark stains that fade before she reaches us. The long curls of her black hair are smoothed back, stuck with the silt-thick water.

The bones of her face shine under the browned skin. She smiles at us.

"Less than this morning. The air's sucking up the water like a sponge. But the Lord will send more. He won't let us thirst."

"Ah, Martha. When He hears your sweet prayers, Martha . . ."

William makes just the inference Martha intends. He dances blindfold, but his steps are perfectly in accord with hers.

We pray for safe conduct until our next stop. Just that. Not even until we reach the next town. Only for the next few

3

hours. Lord be with us.

We walk.

We walk without speaking. We stop often to tie the rags that bind our feet. Except Martha. She walks barefoot on the scorched crust of the earth. The walking does not hurt any longer. Even the child no longer complains. The pain comes when we stop. When we think.

We have been on foot for three days now. Three days and each day beset by a mob, a vile mob. Now there is nothing left for them to steal. Our clothes are gone. We walk in our shifts. Martha wears a padded jacket over hers. It is torn. William covers his nakedness with a beggar's filthy gown. There is nothing left that they could want. But our bodies.

The land has nothing to offer. Each day the riverbed we follow has shown less and less of its dark water. These are the dog days, the *fu-tien*. We have to reach a town. And people.

Martha stops and beckons to James. She crouches down, smiling. I watch as James climbs onto her back. He smiles too now as they pass us.

"The Lord gives you strength, Martha."

"He has framed me to serve Him, William."

She has plastered her voice with piety to please him. She plays the servitor and masters him and he is gratified. A perverse charade — when did it begin?

Martha hails us from our right. James is shouting something and pointing down behind them. We scramble across the rocks. It is only the riverbed James sees. It swings round here.

"Mama, Miss Coleridge found an easy path. You can rest here. And look, there is Chia-hsien; you can see the walls."

And the walls can see us and they can keep us or crush us or spit us out on the other side to the next ring of stone, the next town, the next mob. James, James. It's seven hundred miles to the gunboats and to refuge. Chia-hsien is nothing.

"Yes" — try to smile at him, he's waiting for me to smile — "we'll be at the gates before they close, James."

William thanks the Lord for this uncertain good and we crawl into the shade of an overhang of rock on this barren bluff above this river that isn't there. It is the hottest hour of

4

the day. The heat is still and even here. A clay oven baking the vessels of God.

We close our eyes.

I listen to the rush and hiss of shingle sliding as the wave slopes back to the water massing behind it. I wait for its release under the surge and crash of the next wave. But the water sucks and sucks and the shingle slides and there is nothing to stop it. The hiss is a soft roar and I wake. No shingle, no wave, only the unmistakable sound of approaching feet. Straw sandals shuffling on the dry earth.

The noise grows louder. I wake William and James. Martha has gone. I make William bind the baby tightly against my breast under my shift. His hands are shaking. We step out into the glare of the sun. Martha has gone ahead of us, towards the band of men. She is kneeling again in the stream, modestly this time, humbly.

"Martha sues for our lives."

No, William. Martha sues for her death.

We watch the ragged crowd of men draw nearer. They take shape in the cloud of dust they raise with their shuffling feet. A shoving, muttering apparition, its outline spiked with sticks and spears. And it breaks apart. Some of the men run shouting to the river bank above Martha. James, little James, turns to William but he is staring straight ahead, rigid, whispering through his teeth the same words, over and over.

"Lord, we shall not endure. We shall not endure."

No. Tell the boy something, anything. Help him.

"Your father is praying. Pray with me, James." My lips form the words I think will help the boy. "Be not dismayed for I am thy God; I will strengthen thee." Listen to the words, James. Hear the words. Don't look.

I cover his eyes. The men are hurling stones at Martha where she kneels. They call her a devil-whore. They yell that she lives on the excrement of priests.

But the danger is gone, already it's gone. Look. They won't move. Dear God, they think she's mad. They won't go near her. They won't go near her. Dear God. They're going back.

The mass takes shape again and is one creature advancing with an inhuman growl and the sound of a gong like a brazen heartbeat at its centre. Now we can see the long-pronged tridents of the magistrate's men and my fear is loose inside me. This has all happened before. This time let it be different. Make it be different. Oh God, make it not happen.

The brown hands grab again, tear. Mouths shriek. Limbs lock round us. I feel a weight high on my back and I fall. Fingers jerk at my hair, hauling me up. And let go.

There must have been a signal. The sound of a horn. It's a signal. They're all moving away. We get up, slowly, carefully. Be careful. Don't cry yet, James. Not yet. Look at us. Brushing the dust from these rags, as if it matters.

In front of us is a gaudy sedan. Some official from the magistrate is inside, and he's smiling. After they fell on us like rabble, he's smiling. His speech is hard to understand, convoluted; it sounds prepared. Authority perches precariously on this man. It seems he is our escort into Chia-hsien — another uncertain good.

Beg, then, with civility. Plead with all the obsequiousness we can muster for Martha to accompany us.

He allows her to walk fifty paces behind us. We walk behind the swaying sedan and the jeering and the prodding begin again. Some of the men spit at us. One of them, young and foul-smelling, grabs for my breasts; he starts back when he finds the baby there and a flush spreads quickly under his grimy skin. The others hoot with derision. This retinue is no more than rowdy good-for-nothings.

I look back for Martha. She walks with her head up, her hands swinging slackly at her sides. Black hair, white shift, bare feet on the yellow-brown earth. Biblical. Her eyes are fixed on a point of nothingness. They see nothing. Her expression reminds me of a stereograph we show on the circuit: Christ beatified.

Faith and illusion. Faith and delusion.

Martha Coleridge was not quite what the committee had in mind when they began recruiting. All day I had watched them

6

sitting ramrod straight behind the vast mahogany table, while the applicants filed by, the room growing stuffier and the windows misting higher as the clock ticked on. Something about the operation or the rainy March day seemed to be bringing out all the cranks and misfits in Halifax, pious enough most of them, sincere but sad, hopelessly unfit for the task.

Major Varley was having considerable difficulty staying awake when Martha sailed in, late, not stopping to take off her wrap. She sat before the panel, rainwater dripping from her clothes onto the Indian carpet. She was exultant. And she made it plain: she had to go with us to China.

"I die," she said, sounding not unhappy about it, "I die nightly — nightly — thinking of those millions of souls *starved* of their God."

Over at the desk where I was supposed to be taking notes, I put down my pen and watched as William and the rest of them were stunned into silence by her extravagance.

Martha Coleridge had it all at her fingertips: the barbarism, the heathenism, the poverty and the filth, "the desperate, tongue-blackening thirst for the Savior." At this I had to smile; the marshalled eyebrows of the committee jumped up like caterpillars on a collective string. But there was no stopping her. She quoted the Scriptures.

"Oh, make His name known among the people," she urged the ceiling plaster and for one alarming moment she began to sing, until Major Varley, now wide awake, suggested that a more appropriate occasion might present itself . . . later.

No, Martha certainly was not what they had in mind. Set against the meek and lowly, however, those who might never work themselves up to board the boat, and the zealots who had the gleam of martyrdom in their wild eyes, she was at least promising. She had fervor, that was uncomfortably clear. Her knowledge of the Bible was excellent, of China almost as good. But still I could see what was going on in the minds across the mahogany: there was something untrained about her and perhaps untrainable. She was not quite — decorous.

Among the committee members there was no need for

7

discussion on this point, only a stiffening of spine and tightening of lip, a general closing of the ranks against the unnerving onslaught. They tried evasion tactics. Had Miss Coleridge considered the question of fortitude? They were, they had to admit it, most impressed with her fervor, but in times of trial, and there would be many, would Miss Coleridge find herself sufficient? In a last bid to protect themselves they begged Miss Coleridge to go home and examine the question.

From my place at the desk I could see before any of them the change that came over Martha. The Reverends Hill and Barthelmy were busy rustling papers, and Mr. Perriman was writing himself an intricate note, but William too had seen the change. Major Varley said, "Bye-bye, my dear," and then, "Oh."

Martha was sitting stock-still.

She waited until she had their attention and then she looked each of them straight in the eye. She looked for a long time.

William coughed nervously.

"Gentlemen," she said, "are you suggesting I respond to God with a question? I have a calling; we all here have a calling but now you would like me to question mine. You're asking me in effect to question God's judgement. Well, gentlemen, I am not so bold. Refuse me if you like but don't ask me to refuse my God."

Martha used her logic like a blunt instrument. It achieved her object — and more; William never has recovered from the blow.

I look back again. This time Martha sees me and smiles and I sicken. It is the idiot beam of the martyr.

"William, make them stop. Martha should be with us."

"At least we're all alive. Be careful what you say, Emily."

I shake William's hand from my arm and hurry forward to the side of the sedan to speak to the retainer, a half-starved looking fellow with broken teeth. He looks at me not unkindly but shakes his head. I ask to go down the stream bed and I show him that Mercy, awake now at my breast, has fouled her wrappings. He laughs and I get my way. The whole retinue stops for one incontinent infant. As I had hoped, no one protests Martha's approach. The men are no longer interested. Madness is her own dirty baby at her breast; like maternity it is not attractive for long.

When we set off again some of the men remain but others break away, leaving the road and taking a shorter route to the town so that our escort, if that is what it is, is diminished. The curtains on the official chair are closed. Martha walks with us now, her vacant, holy stare interrupted by the need to help James. She is singing softly to him, trying to take his mind off his tiredness. He, poor lamb, has lost all heart; even his crying sounds perfunctory.

As we approach the gates the gong sounds again and men and boys run out. Some inside have climbed the stone stairs to the top of the walls, black against the faded mauve of the late day. The remnants of our escort blow horns and bang tinny cymbals for the official's entrance and the discordant notes mix with the din of the crowd about the gates. We walk closer together. The people press on every side as we pass under the tower that crowns the gate. We cling together now as if we are caught in a rising tide. Martha sings more and more loudly as our pace slows. Then she is separated from us, torn away by the press of bodies and caught up in a side stream back towards the gate. I can hear her voice rising above the noise of the crowd. The words of the hymn ring against the stone. I look back and she is there, baring her throat as if for air, singing with a power to burst her lungs. The people have drawn back in a ring, recoiled from her unlikely presence like water from a stone. She is her own protection.

James is screaming, "No, no! Stop them! Stop them!" But the rough hands are on us again, trying with their shoving to salvage some authority, and we are pushed on towards the yamen. How to explain to James in his terror? Martha's body is not in danger from these people. Even William's repetition of "the Lord will protect her" is unnecessary. They are rowdies only; they look for fools, not victims, want their amusement but at no risk. They will not touch.

No, Martha, your body is safe enough despite all you do

— *yes, I have seen* — to destroy it. But your soul, Martha, why are you damning your soul?

We reach the walls that enclose the yamen in the guts of the town. Inside — inside? The workings of officialdom seethe or stagnate on an unpredictable diet of ordinances from Peking. The colored sedan is disappearing through the gates.

We follow.

James is already asleep, his face dreamless, his limbs quiet. I settle down with Mercy to wait for William. The room is almost bare, a wooden door, a brick floor stepped up to a dais of brick for sleeping, a gutter running along the base of one wall to drain in the corner, a latticed window high up. *Is* it a cell? There is a large ewer of clean water beside a shallow stone basin. The ewer is as comforting as a fat matron. In this time of drought it can mean only goodwill.

We have been clothed and fed, there is that. A servant brought clean clothes, for me a padded blue jacket and trousers, the same for James, for William the long, straight gown of a scholar. The servant waited while we changed and he took away our filthy rags. Then a girl — his wife? — came with things for the baby. Together we bathed Mercy, dressed her in the small coat embroidered with flowers, but all the time the girl kept her eyes away from mine and would not speak. Not a word.

They brought us food, too: bowls of dumplings in broth, a dish of steaming millet, tea. James ate like a pig and burnt his mouth. We all ate like pigs, only silently. The servant came back to clear the empty, shining bowls from the floor. When he left he let fall the bar on the outside of the heavy wooden door. William said it was for our protection.

"Everything is for the best."

Did he believe that? And if he didn't believe it, whose faith was he bolstering? Mine? His? And faith in what — our safety, the Lord, the Word? Or faith in himself? Words used not to be necessary for that. He was unshakable. Now he dumps his phrases round us like sandbags against the siege. Against your fear isn't it, William? You know it's there, like rats outside

10

your barricades, gnawing. Your words grains of sand, useless, trickling away to nothing.

Words. William said that the magistrate quite plainly recognised his official rank: an ordained, medical missionary, at least equal to a district magistrate. The Imperial edict last year had confirmed it. And in any event, he said, the magistrate was a high-ranking scholar, someone who knew intelligence and education when he saw it. Oh, yes, he saw it all right. They wouldn't have any difficulty getting along. No difficulty at all.

All this bluff and bravado, but his doubts as palpable as intruders in a darkened house. When the guard came to summon him, William stopped at the door to pray, turning his back on him as he would to a servant. He asked God to make the people understand the great benefit that would come to them from helping us, His servants. But he prayed aloud, in Mandarin.

Am I supposed to believe in you, William, now, your own faith all in shreds?

There was a time. There was a time . . .

The whole world was in movement. Clouds were massing, bits of twig spinning and slipping away in the fast stream. We lay by the willows on the banks of the Mourne at Auldbury. The surface of the water darkening with the changing light, and every blade of grass on the bank shuddering with it. There were elms on the other side, their leaves quaking, turning bright bellies against the advancing sky.

Only William was firm, fixed against all the quick movement.

"It's the greatest cause I can think of, I know that. God's own work. You couldn't ask for more." His resolution grave and solid, sunk in bedrock conviction but in the dazzling light transfigured, shot through with courage, a vision. I longed for him to ask me to go with him and when he did I loved him.

On the train with him bound for Vancouver I had already forgotten the willows with their long branches fingering and feathering the current as it slid from them. Gray-green leaves flickering against the wind.

I hear footsteps, the jangling voice of the guard, a thud as the bar is slid back. And there is Martha, solemn but resigned, pausing in the doorway to thank the guard — composed, as if she were coming into church. She wears a man's quilted jacket and beneath it a voluminous European skirt of perhaps thirty years ago.

Martha. Safe. We both smile and it feels like crying.

Then Martha tells, briefly, how a man fell from the wall, how the mob took fright at that, believing their own cries of "Devil" to be true, how, as she made her way to the yamen, watched from doorways and from alleys, she was stopped and drawn into a tiny courtyard. There was an old man there, ashamed to see her pitiful condition. He gave her his jacket and the ancient skirt — the gift, or the loss, of some itinerant missionary years ago. This sudden compassion — it runs through these people, twin river to their quick cruelty, beyond understanding.

Someone comes with food for Martha. Our status, then, has not changed. While she eats I explain that William has an audience with the magistrate. He will clarify our position and perhaps even offer assistance. I hear no pious droppings from Martha in reply, no prayers for divine intercession. She simply nods; licks her bowl; urinates without apology in the stone gutter; takes off the wide skirt and rolls it for a pillow. Then she curls up like a child on the brick and is asleep immediately.

Yes, she has strength, but it has nothing at all to do with what they wanted in Halifax: fortitude — that suitably, decorously spiritual, stiff upper lip, that quality that would raise us above this heathen mess and make it all supportable. Martha hasn't any use for that, even though she puts it on from time to time, like whalebone, for William. She endures by strength, physical strength. She has an animal instinct for survival that makes her suicidal gestures — in the river, at the gate — inexplicable.

William thinks they were acts of courage, those lunatic stances. He said they were ploys to let us get away to safety. No. Martha is wrapped inside herself. She turns in, curls in, as if she would consume her own soul. Her struggle is private and does not admit of our existence. She is living inside herself. She doesn't even feel the fly there crossing and recrossing her eyelid. Only her nerves twitch, like the skin on the backs of mules. She doesn't wake.

This isn't Martha sleeping greedily here.

The day we sailed — how cross William was with Martha then.

"Miss Coleridge seems to make a habit of being late," he said, always ready to detect a pattern in occurrences numbering more than one, and growing colder by the minute on the greasy quay.

The *Empress of China* towered above us, cutting out the last of the sun. Her cargo was almost loaded and the guests were streaming from her like outcasts from the ark. It was almost five o'clock. At the hotel that morning Martha had promised to meet us again at three.

Having succeeded in reaching Vancouver without incident, William could not imagine anything more unimaginable than missing the boat. "You go on board, my dear," he said, his foot on the gangplank, when Martha's hansom came careening into view. Loath to relinquish his physical contact with the boat in case the thing should actually sail, William nevertheless hurried over to help Martha down from the cab.

"Oh, Dr. Bancroft, I can't wait," she said, "I can't wait to get started, can you?"

William found himself unable to answer.

Our party was small.

There were, besides Martha and ourselves, another couple on their first China mission, a Reverend Pritchard and his somewhat peevish wife, and the sanguine Dr. Willis, an old China hand of vast experience and an insatiable desire to recount it.

"You'll have no use for those," he said to Martha when she showed us that evening what had kept her so long in Vancouver. We were in the forward saloon and Martha had laid out her new books on the table — *Forty Years in the Field,*

13

Saving the Middle Kingdom, and one or two other earnest testaments.

"You'll learn everything you need to know by doing it. If I were you I'd throw them overboard," he said without realizing she would take his statement quite so literally.

"Shall we take a turn on the deck?" she said on our way back to our cabins that evening, and before I knew it she was at the rail and the wind was glancing through the pages of *Forty Years in the Field* before they disappeared in the foam.

By the time we were six days out Martha had converted half the crew ("Crew," said Mrs. Pritchard, "ought not to be allowed above the engine room"), if not to God then at least to attendance at her boat-deck meetings. They came whenever they could, but brought with them motives that grubbied their souls before the first hymn had been sung.

I went to one of those meetings. I saw the men with their hard eyes staring, staring as if they could see her body under the woollen dress. I saw one of them run his tongue across his lips. I knew and the captain knew. After a while he withdrew his permission. There were those of us who were greatly relieved.

Martha was not at all discouraged. When we reached Shanghai she carried with her intact the absolute conviction that happiness could be spread around, distributed, rather like the loaves and the fishes, and armed with that conviction she took to the streets at once, noisy, smelly, dirty though they were.

Down at the waterfront, among the market people and the tradesmen and the rough coolies, she practised her phrases and handed out tracts and smiles; she talked her way into the confidence of the food vendors; she attracted crowds where business was thin. Sometimes in the evening she came back to the Institute with all the tracts still under her arm but with the smiles stuck like handbills over the faces of everyone she had met. It was at the waterfront that she began to learn the language and the customs — and not a few of the quirks — of these people she had come to save, and for it she won the firm disapproval of the more conservative members of the

14

Institute.

We had our learning managed neatly for us by an amiable teacher in a comfortable classroom and for this we were grateful. We studied the language, carefully keeping our heads down, delved into the intricacies of Chinese etiquette, contemplated the problem of the three religions. And while we sat we wondered what possessed Martha to walk for hours, enduring no end of familiarities and unpleasantness — not to mention the rain.

In private conversations we answered our own question: what possessed Miss Coleridge, what drove her, was that slightly unstable streak that had tweaked the eyebrows of the Halifax committee. Of course, there was no real reason to ask her to stop what she was doing; it was, after all, what she had come to China for in the first place. It fell to me, nevertheless, to speak to her.

I took her aside one evening after dinner and began lamely. Didn't she find it awfully difficult working alone out there where there was so much noise and confusion? No, she didn't find it difficult at all. In fact, Miss Coleridge didn't seem to find anything difficult or worrying or daunting. And as our conversation progressed it became clear that she didn't find anything improvident, or imprudent, or inappropriate either. In fact — here Martha took hold of my hand in both her own — she had always meant to ask me to join her. Wouldn't I? Wouldn't I really? I should love it. Miss Coleridge knew I should.

I left wishing I had said yes.

The next morning Martha was out early as usual. Shanghai was teeming with a relentless rain.

The heat is unbearable in this room. And why don't they come back with William? There is no sleeping, but it's not the heat, not even the convulsive movements I feel beginning inside me, keeping me awake: it's Martha.

Martha. My eyes turn back and back to her curled and fetal body. The thought of Martha crawls over my brain like a louse on my scalp. I scratch and scratch but still it slips away

15

and still it crawls. But this *is* Martha sleeping here. Elemental. No more layers to hide the core. Something all at once has stripped her to the bone, taken faith, taken hope and left her flayed.

Something. But not this trouble we are in. No, because she has suffered more than this. In Shansi, at Jun-ch'eng, there was worse — but it didn't destroy her. Not like this. She kept what she needed, everything that made her a little crazy, yes, but still alive, still living in soul and body and, God help her, still human. This is different.

Then the louse creeps back again. Why? For survival? Then I could understand. But it isn't that. Martha hasn't thrown away all her trappings, all her human kindness only to run; Martha has been walking in all her nakedness straight to her assailants. Why? Why when she has cut right down to the core of brute self-preservation does she turn around and invite her own destruction?

I hear voices at the door. William is in the passage. Martha starts awake and draws on her skirt. Why, why, why in the midst of our dire need, does Martha, living now only in her body, take the trouble to compose her features and replace the brutish, empty resignation with pious forbearance? For *him*? William is shown in. He sees Martha and goes to her first, greeting her as if she were Lazarus risen.

Both the children rouse from their sleep and James speaks at once. "May we go now?"

Nobody answers.

I find it difficult to repeat his question for him. William is still holding Martha's hands in his. "Well, William?"

"In a moment, Emily. First I have to hear what miracle preserved our dear friend here."

Interesting, how concerned he is now. You said the Lord would protect her, William, when you were in the thick of it. That was enough for you at the time.

Martha repeats her story briefly for William. "And now tell us, Dr. Bancroft. Has the Lord heard our prayers at last?" But we know the answer already by William's silence. We knew as soon as he walked in without a fanfare of his success.

16

"Well, ladies, we must wait and see."

"But you saw him, the magistrate?"

"Oh, yes, I saw him. Fine man. A *chü-jen*, you know, an M.A. Treated me with a fair amount of respect, I can tell you. Oh, yes, we had a long talk."

"But is he going to help us?"

"Oh, no doubt, no doubt. He's conferring right now with his secretary on how to get us to Hsiang-ch'eng. It's seventeen miles, you know. Southeast, I think he said. Oh, a very accommodating sort."

"Then we leave tomorrow?"

"Provided all the arrangements have been made, yes, Emily."

"What arrangements? William, are we at liberty?"

"I believe we're free to go to Hsiang-ch'eng, yes."

"But are we free?"

William sighs. He's looking at me with controlled exasperation; I might be James wheedling for something he knows he can't have.

"Now you know it's not as easy as that. Matters are arranged quite differently here. You know that. Some things you just don't ask a district magistrate, not unless you want to insult him and, speaking for myself, Emily, I'm not prepared to go that far." He turns to Martha. "At least you're safe. And no more reckless gestures, I hope. Not for us at any rate. We're all equal in the eyes of the Lord, all equally valuable . . ."

I try not to listen to William and Martha arousing each other to heights of humility. Turn my attention to the children. Put Mercy's nuzzling, rooting face to my breast.

James comes over. "She's hungry."

"She's always hungry."

"I want to sit on your lap."

Fed and rested and clothed, now he remembers his mother's arms. Stronger than any of us, he puts his needs in an order of strict priority and concentrates on each in turn. When all are filled he is satisfied. It is quite simple. And if the memory of the want remains, it is harmless; he doesn't think to look forward, not like us. We are possessed by the need to look forward. We look forward and so we know and the knowing destroys us.

"Tell me a story, James."

"No, you tell, Mama. Tell about Grampa's house."

Yes, I'd like to tell about that. I'd like to take you there, little rabbit, let you run free in the salty wind.

"Well, first you have to imagine the Atlantic. It's awfully big."

He doesn't believe it can be wider than this miserable plain. And it's hard to describe its cold, glinting expanse, the force of the waves as they fall on the shingle. Impossible to give him the excitement of white clouds bowling high above the breaking waves, gulls screaming, the wind rushing through the coarse grass on the low, crumbling cliffs.

While I try to tell him these things my mind plunges and sheers back to the afternoon at the Cove when William and I scrambled hand in hand up the steps in the cliff face, scrambled back towards the house so that there would be time. So that there would be time enough.

James is asleep now. William takes him and lays him carefully on his jacket. Then he lies down beside him. I stretch out, keeping Mercy on the crook of my arm, and listen to the breathing in the room. Martha is already asleep again. William awake. I want to be back on the cliffs, gasping and hurrying with William, the wind catching our breath.

We had left old Doctor Bancroft and the others walking.

"Slow down. They'll be an age yet."

"I can't slow down."

We had said we would go back ahead of them to have the tea prepared. We slowed down on the gravel walk across the lawn. William went to give the orders to the kitchen while I waited for him upstairs. In the darkness of my room I lay on the bed and stroked the inside of my thighs so that I would be ready. So that he could not be too quick.

It was always like that in those weeks after our marriage, always secret, hurried, illicit. Perhaps because we were in the houses of our childhood. Or perhaps because William was William.

18

He said on our wedding night that we shouldn't abuse the gift of love, shouldn't misdirect our energies, squander our strength. But even as he spoke I saw the muscles of his face and neck tense and heard his voice thicken with saliva. There was not time even to remove the wedding gown. Later he apologized and, gently then, entered me again, showing me how it could be, and again, far into the night.

In the morning he asked me to join him on his knees to pray to the Lord for more restraint. I smiled. William was nothing but a chicken-thief knocking at the farmhouse door, pledging his reform and all the while eyeing the flurry of feathers in the coop, compounding the theft with a promise about to be broken. It seemed like such a complicated sin, scarcely worth the bother.

But the next night William was watching the hands of the clock in the corner for the hour when we could decently retire. I knew what he was thinking and pictured it all again, the muscle, the sweat, the hair. And then the memory of his touch returned. By the time William came to me again in my room, I was weak with wanting and it was over almost as soon as it was begun. And when he was still I asked him to go on and he found ways to please me until I pressed my face deep into the mattress to keep from crying out.

After that, the thought of it was always there. There was no undoing it; it was like a secret betrayed. As for abstention, William had no success at all in keeping his resolve. His weakness disturbed him. As a safeguard, he began to go out of his way to look for company, he would encourage walks with his father and my sisters, arrange rides, picnics. Then, while his father scanned the bright air for larks, while Florence fussed about the way the preserves attracted wasps and while Dora wiped her children's faces, then our eyes would search each other out and some pretext, not a lie, would fly to his tongue and we would leave the party for the curtained dimness of my room.

Decency demanded that we should not stay away for long, should not disturb the bed, should stifle our noise. Decency made us indecent. We reached into each other's clothing, we

19

piled pillows on the carpet, we stood, we knelt. And we learned the placing of our bodies that would most swiftly, and most quietly, bring each other to an end.

I open my eyes. It is dark. Our small lamp has burnt out. There is a noise outside, a confusion. The others are stirring. The noise grows louder. The shuffling feet again. And the hissing. There is a great clamor in the courtyard. Martha calls tentatively to the guard. He's still there. She asks him to light our lamp. A mistake: as soon as the lamp glows, a cry goes up outside. A stone is hurled, breaking through the paper and wooden lattice of the high window. The hissing becomes a word spat and spat again.

"Sha! Sha! Sha!" Kill. Kill. Kill.

The guard does not know what is happening. He's too frightened to answer us. It must be the end. There's no other way. We are martyrs to official bungling. We're caught here. In this trap. Not even the mission compound or the altar steps, William. Not even the market place, Martha. Here in this mundane little room, this hole — this trap.

We kneel together, facing the door, our backs shielding the children still asleep, and the hissing becomes a shriek. There are sounds on the outside wall. We look up to the small window with the broken paper and wait for whomever is climbing to frame himself there. A face appears. The voice screams at us. The mouth spits through blackened teeth. The eyes are almost closed with hatred. Now gone. The eyes flew open at the last word as he fell away.

There must be soldiers out there, trying to gain control. We stop praying. We try to distinguish the sounds and decipher their meaning. The chant is ebbing. The first convulsion of panic leaves us. Martha is standing up, smoothing out the skirt. She is saying she will go outside to speak with them. William is saying we must each do as the Lord bids us. Let her go? Would he really let her go out there?

"No Martha. Are you mad?" I catch at her arm.

"The Lord will tell us what to say."

"Martha, you'll be struck down before you have time to

speak."

She's saying something about God's will. I feel anger, a pain in my chest, in my throat. I begin to shout: "God's will? Whose God? Our Liar-God? He's done nothing for us. He's deserted us. He has no right to ask for our deaths. You idiot. You fool."

The brick floor against my face. I feel Martha and William holding my arms. I hear my own voice draining away, trickling through the joins in the brick.

I hear Martha's voice, deep and calm. "I'll stay, William. I can be more use here."

James is crying. Quiet now, I untangle myself and go to him. He must not see the monster of my fear again. But it's out. It's loose now and I feel it ranging round me. It is shaggy with images of the massacre at Shang-te fu. When the news reached us — when, ten days ago, eleven — we didn't speak about it but acted only, piling everything we could on the great cart, flying from Tsehchow, flying to Martha and sweeping her up with us, flying on and hurtling, hurtling down the broken rubbled mountains to this endless plain.

No, we didn't speak about it, the news of the massacre. We didn't speak but each of us pictured, *saw*.

William is praying. Martha beside him bows her head. I repeat my own private litany: I fear for our lives; I fear for our children; I fear death; I fear pain; I fear the agony of the flesh and the soul-drowning grief of despair; I fear to hear my children cry for help and to be helpless; I fear to hear my children cry . . .

William is praying. Martha is praying.

I sit. I sit with my legs drawn up to my chest and I rock.

A trial! God in Heaven. That wasn't a trial. It was a fiasco, a travesty of all that's civilized. Hauled out of here for the sake of a mob, a frustrated mob, and verbally mauled in the official presence of the magistrate. Accusations, abuse, insults, lies, fantasies. And he with his pale, blank face, sitting there, careful not to disturb the scrupulous arrangement of his yards of brocade, nodding to his scribe flicking the black marks of our

21

death over the paper, not listening, planning only, contriving how to get rid of us, with honor. William's educated man! So educated, so highly advanced that now we stand convicted of obscene practices with converts, of collecting the eyes of children to grind for medicine, of befouling temples, stealing clothes and holding off the rains.

Convicted.

Sentenced.

Flung back in this room to wait for it and no one to tell us how it will be done.

William. You could have done something. Nothing to barter or bribe with, but there are other ways. Flattery, promises, lies. You could have tried. Connived, conspired, recanted. Anything. But you didn't — wouldn't. Standing there letting your useless, watery words dribble from the corners of your mouth: "We are humble servants, only, of our Master. We wish you no harm."

Well *I* wish the mandarin monkey harm. I shouldn't mind seeing his head set up in a cage on his own walls. I'd be happy. So you see, William, you ended by lying, after all. You might as well have lied to some purpose, invented some useful deception, something, at least, to extricate us from this ungodly mess. If God gave us nothing else to live by, He at least gave us our wits; the weapons of our survival. And you stood there witless.

But it's done and nothing — not even prayers — can change it now. It's final. An end to it. And I could be glad. If it were for me only I could be glad. I could be like Martha, suicidal. Seek it out, long for it. But for the children? And not know how? This magistrate is a danger to us even now. Prevaricating old fool. Our deaths may be as muddled and as sickening as our trial. Oh God, take care of the children! But if they cry for help? And no one answers? And James thinks I have forsaken him and let them hurt him?

No. Ah, my sweet loves, no. I can show you more mercy than this God of ours.

If only William were asleep now, like Martha, deep in her dreams of death. But he is still kneeling. Waiting or praying.

22

And the room is too bright. They took our lamp away when they took the water, but the moon flares steadily, white through the broken window.

But William has his back to me and I could still do it if I were quick enough, strong enough. And James not struggle. Yes, if James is the first. Mercy would blow her life away on a breath, but James — James must be first, before I lose courage.

They shan't harm you, my Jamie. Feel. No pain. The jacket I have folded for you, a soft pad against your cheek. There. On your face. The softness. No blows. You don't move. You understand it all, don't you? The need, the love. You know not to wake. Feel. Comfort of darkness, drying all the tears, closing out the day — "Let him sleep, Emily."

My own breath stops. I cannot move. William's voice echoes round inside my head but does not die away. Let him sleep. Let him sleep. The words are all I have. I am empty. I took my soul between my hands to cover James's face and now it's gone. I can do nothing now. There is nothing.

"Come away and pray, Emily."

But I cannot move from James's side. William comes and draws me away. He prays. His words fly about the empty room as they did inside my head. Words about forgiveness and mercy. Words about salvation and peace. But I cannot pray. I cannot. The words that clack over and over on my tongue in my closed mouth say only, "Make it be over. Make it be over."

The wood is scored with the long streaks of its own grain. Our eyes stare and stare at its dark oiled surface. I begin to think of Auldbury, of the table in the cool kitchen. It too was scored, its grain deepened into long grooves and ribs by years of scrubbing. But it was white, bleached by the lye. And soft. Even a child's fingernails were harder, could pick away the ribs. "Emmie! My table!" Mrs. Gale turns, halfway to the stove with her pan of plums. And I am nine years old again, trying to say I want to stay, my stomach seasick with suspense as I wait, away from my bags in the hall, hoping that the hour

23

will pass when I must kiss mother goodbye, knowing she will come at any moment, and the certain knowing becomes more certain and there is nothing I can do and my tears make sandy colored patches on the white wood.

But now there is no nervous picking with fingernails; and this wood is solid and black. So we sit in the cart, waiting for these gates to open, staring at the dark wood.

There is nothing to do but wait. No one is going to tell us why the guards came before dawn, why we left the yamen by a private door. We do not know — nor shall we ask — why we were led past the west gate, past — oh, God — past the place of execution. The mule-cart was waiting, guarded at the south gate. We stopped and the guards pushed us onto it. We saw the water gourd, then the basket of millet and the iron kettle. When James began shouting, "A journey! It's a journey . . ." I clapped my hand over his mouth, not wanting to trust such a fragile hope to that chill hour before dawn.

And so we don't speak about it. We sit here in this cart, before these massive gates and we wait. The mules nod between the traces. The guards speak across us. James has fallen asleep under his father's arm, Mercy against my breast, bound tightly there. Opposite me sits Martha watching the eastern sky, her face clear and untroubled.

I hear sounds from the darkness of an archway. Two beggars wrapped in their filthy sleeping blankets and not much more stumble out onto the cobbles. They stop and confer, perhaps conspire, come towards us, grinning, palms held out. To beg or to mock? The guards turn to look at them jabbering at us beside the cart. The nearest guard prods at them half-heartedly with his trident. They move away a little distance. Strangely their presence does not make me uneasy, or apprehensive, or even indignant, and the action of the guards leaves me indifferent. I am not moved to gratitude or relief. Nothing can move me now. I have only to sit and wait. We have all only to sit and wait. Fear and hope are equally unsafe in this hour, at this gate, and so we wrap ourselves in a blanket of unfeeling against the chill and we wait.

There are more beggars round us, tainting the sharp air

with their foul breath and the stench of their rags. The guards make desultory attempts to move them back. Not one of us has moved. I look at Martha facing me. She inclines her head, opening her eyes wide and indicating with her glance the eastern sky behind me. I turn and see it suffused with greenish-pink. The horizon is a black line.

The gatekeeper shuffles from his house. He is old, crooked. Bent nearly in two, he shuffles with his head down. He shows no sign of noticing the beggars or the guards or us but goes straight with the giant key to the iron lock and pulls back the massive doors. With a thin scream the two wooden wheels of our cart begin to roll.

The backs of the mules steam as the sun rises higher. Their hooves beat a complicated rhythm on the packed earth. Look back. The beggar men string out along the road, flakes of blue against the singed land. There is a clarity to the air that has washed the whole country as far as the mountains in front of us. Thin clouds lift like smoke from their tops. Nothing to do but be carried along by the screeching wheels.

Try not to think of the heat that will come. Coolness. If only it would last.

Green. Think of green. The place under the willows where moss clung round the boles, even in summer. A root that slid out over the water. Green shade where I used to sit swinging my feet in the glossy stream until Florrie shrilled at me from the house: "E-mi-*ly*! Mother says *now*!" And then Mother's voice: "That will *do*, Florence. Don't be so *loud*!" I would pick up my damp stockings and trail back up to the house.

And green leaves under the green glass of the conservatory. Plants there slick-leaved and shiny in their china pots and a little yellow-tiled pool in the centre with water cool and clear and just shallow enough for scooping up the colored pebbles, making it gulp and swallow them again.

Then dark green under the yew. Dark like the green in the black of a starling's wing. A secret place for a child to slip under the flat branches, to watch fears and dreams mushroom ghostly pale in the dark, to stare into its shadows, consider the magic of its poisonous berry. And one day, the day that Father collapses, a dropped sack on the cobbles of the stableyard, run there, to the yew, and lie there afraid to move; and look at the berries and think about my own mouth round the small waxy fruit, and take one and taste and not die; then swallow and still not die, though I lie there and lie there until the green turns to blue.

And the blackbird — I had forgotten. It sang in the evening, in summer, from the plum tree nearest the house while I lay inside, not sleeping, watching the liquid blue sky and seeing the notes of its birdsong as they rippled across, tiny brilliant leaves, fluttering across the fading blue.

"Mother," I said once, "do you know the blackbird's song is bright green?"

"Your conversation is so often foolish it's tedious," she said, and she hauled *Nature's Kingdom* off the shelf so that I could read her the section on domestic birds. I was still copying in the afternoon when Father asked me what I was doing.

"Green," he said. "I think you're right, Emmie. It's certainly not mauve like the smell of the honeysuckle."

After he died, Auldbury was never the same. I felt always there was something I had forgotten to do, someone I had forgotten to see; no time to tell him goodbye.

The day after he fell, the day that Mother drew me from the kitchen, handed me into the carriage, that day, they said he was sleeping. They said he was certain to see the honeysuckle I picked for his room. "As soon as he wakes, dear." They said he would send to thank me. "Yes, dear, his note will reach you at Uncle Samuel's the very same day that he sends."

The note was important. I held the idea of it tightly all the way as if I already had it in my hands, and I waited, the noise and the bustle of the strange household spinning around the emptiness of the note not coming.

"Uncle Samuel, do you think Father's been called back to the circuit? Sometimes, you know, they need a preacher really badly."

Uncle Samuel looked at me hard. Then he patted my cheek and answered in lies.

As I lie to James.

But I knew. Not the words, only the unformed knowledge. All the weeks that I stayed there, held apart from the truth but knowing it, the sense of it anyway, like someone present in a dark room, I longed to hear the thing that I dreaded. And on my way back, I knew. When we rounded the drive and I saw the drawn curtains, when my mother, nun-like, led me inside, I knew. But still I had to ask and had to hear the words. And the words told me there would have been time.

Ah, no reproach. What does it matter now? All our lives wasted and useless. William's paid out steadily to his smug parishioners until he drops to the stones of his own stableyard. And mine? Mrs. William Bancroft of Nova Scotia, sent here to founder on a burning plain. And for what? For love, I used to think. But now my tongue sucks at the side of my mouth with hatred for these heathens. My brothers.

The freshness of the dawn evaporates. The cart jolts more sharply it seems. Its wheels screech more loudly. The rabble that has followed at a distance draws in closer. The flies come from nowhere to plague us again. And the heat builds, adding stifling weight to the oppression that has borne down on me since William drew my hand away from James's sleeping face. But the others too, I see, give themselves up to the jolt and lurch of the cart and stare blankly into the glare of the morning. Nothing to do but wish each step from the town to be one hundred across this everlasting ochre-colored plain.

Go back. Go back again to Auldbury. To the glossy browns and the cool greens, winding rivers and shaded banks; the path that led up from the quiet Mourne to the house, all leafy and tangled in summer; the big veranda where the wooden chairs stood waiting for us; the conversations that mingled and twined in the mauve-scented evening while the smooth surface of the Mourne slid away under the willows . . .

A horn sounds from the walls of the town behind us. The guard with the lead mule hears it and stops. "Take, take," he says to William, handing him the rope. The beggars see this and begin to jabber excitedly. The two guards, without another word or even a glance at us, are turning back to the town. Some of the beggars are already reaching down to pick up stones at the side of the road. William's voice rises as they come forward.

"Lord, show us the way."

The mules balk, will not go on. I reach forward for the bamboo goad. Hands on my outstretched arm. Crash of hard earth up to my face. The breath out of me and searing back in one long ache while the hands claw at my clothes and twist my arms and legs out of them ... and the bindings at my breast ... and my baby is gone.

Crawl. Get to her. Hot earth and stones scrape my knees and elbows but I cannot reach the thieves or the cart. And the guards, though they do not look back, the guards know what is happening behind them.

I see the wheels high in the air. The mules run free with their honking, sawing cry across the flat land beside the road and three men run shrieking and yelling behind them. The wheels fall from the sky and the cart is righted again. The scattered thieves gather to it. A purpose grows in their confusion. They turn the cart back the way we have come and it begins, under their hands, to roll, forward, towards me, over the scattered rags they have flung from their foul bodies.

A bundle is moving. It squirms.

"William! William! The baby!" Dear God. William, move! Save her! But William is face down, lying still. The cart is rolling, lurching. Out of reach. The hands pushing. Feet trampling. Mercy wriggling in its path.

Martha. She throws herself across the bundle, flattening into the yellow dust. The cart jerks once as it hits her back then rolls again, one of the great wheels riding high, humping up and over, tilting the cart until it crashes down by her shoulder, hitting an incline, making the beggars shriek and yell as they run with it past me back to the city.

I crawl forward.

Martha is slowly getting up. She turns her head to the dry brown grass that stretches away to one side of the road.

"James!"

28

The grass ripples and parts and James's white face shows in the rustling brown. He darts out like a rabbit. I help Martha to her feet and I see that Mercy, thank God, is still breathing. She whimpers. I put her to my bare breast, hold her there and she quiets.

William is sitting up. He holds his head. James, my little rabbit, stands beside him, eyes wide, silent, willing him, as I am, to get up, to be Papa again. We gather the rags the beggars discarded and cover ourselves as best we can. James takes some to William. At last William rouses himself and we go down the bank to the riverbed. A thin line marks the place where the water coursed between the rocks. A thin line of earth colored darker than the rest of the silted yellow bed. There is no water.

Only James speaks about it, later. He states simply that he is thirsty and no one chides him. He knows none of the implications, is innocent of despair. He might be one of Dora's children on a July afternoon. Lemonade served in the shade of the elm.

We have sat and stared at the dry course but we haven't moved. Our mouths are too dry even to cleanse our cuts and grazes. We sit. William does not give thanks that we live. We can look forward but we cannot know. The next town is close, twelve miles perhaps. Close enough for rumors to fly there before us, condemn us before we arrive.

The rains are long overdue. They must come. Two months they have been expected. Tomorrow they could begin. We could wait. I do not know what color the sky is. It flares and beats above us. Brightness. The color of brightness. It gives only heat.

"We'd better move."

Martha is right. It's madness to be out here where the rocks shout back at the sun and our breath is sucked out of us by the empty air.

"No, Mama, Papa. Let's not go. Please."

"We can't stay here, Jamie."

"I don't want to go. I want to wait for the river to come back."

29

"It's not going to do that, my love."

"Not even if we ask God?"

I tell him we must find shelter first. Then we will dig for water. Is that wicked — to offer him hope, when there is none; to offer him lies? What else can I do?

Walking, we find our strength again. Almost all around us is flat. No shade. There is an outcrop of rocky ground ahead. Shadows perhaps, hidden in its sides. We walk in silence. The hill can be reached.

William walks ahead. Anyone watching would say he's leading us, but his step is hesitant, faltering. He wasn't particularly hurt in the attack; it's his faith that is halting. He should be a prophet walking here in this desert place. Yes, John. Rags flapping about the great white bones of his arms and legs. His face when he turns to wait for us blackened with his beard that is growing through, his hair standing thick and wild from his head. But his eyes are not the eyes of a prophet. No shaft of fire. Fear escapes from them like blood from a wound.

There was a time.

There was a time. In Lin-an. It was how I always wanted it. William burning then and nothing to stop him.

Lin-an had been tried before. They'd sent others there; the Board had seen it as a likely foothold. But they'd turned back, the ones who had been sent before. Not William — nothing discouraged William. The rabble at the gates, the soldiers round the yamen, the mandarin's advisers, and the mandarin himself were powerless.

"Righteousness and truth: we need no more armor than that."

And then, believing in him, I believed in everything. Courage from conviction. Yes, there was a time. In Lin-an, William, do you remember? How you outfaced the mob there? How you climbed up on the balustrade of the compound steps, swinging me up beside you, and preached to the crowd right there, shocking them into silence, into submission? Do you?

And you told me how the mandarin had stared in astonishment on our arrival when you demanded your rights

30

at your very first meeting. But he knew you were strong and he feared you. His smiling face and his soft voice opened doors in the town; he found us the compound, gave us his cards — while his agents stirred up the verminous dregs of the gutters against us.

I remember, William. I remember how none of it mattered because you believed. And I trusted.

I remember the room. It was bare. The furniture all at the doors for a barricade. I remember the heat. The shutters had been closed all day. And Martha and I waiting. Then you slipped back unseen into the house and though you had run through the streets and alleys like a criminal there wasn't a trace of fear on your face. You had sent runners off in three directions, remember? You said you knew one of the messages, a telegram, something, would get through to the gunboats. You'd bribed them. I think you'd threatened them. You were very certain.

"There's not a thing can harm us. Not a thing."

And the room was bare. There was only a candle. And we didn't light it. And we didn't pray. Martha next door fast asleep and we lying together in the heat and listening to the murmurings and gatherings outside. Then when the noises outside massed into a roar and Martha was calling and we smelled the smoke from the burning torches, then, only then did you get up, dress, and go outside to face them, your voice shaking with fury not fear, bludgeoning them into submission. They looked in your eyes and mistook what they saw there for what they had feared to see, the living God, and they were afraid.

No. What they saw there was you, William. You should be with us now. That figure that lay, uninjured, his face in the dust while the cart bore down on our baby . . . that wasn't you.

Ah, fearless. I remember. The street all quiet and we already sleeping again when the men from the gunboat, perplexed, knocked at the door.

I shift Mercy against my breast and she shudders. My little, my pretty. I do not thank God for your life. I do not. I have not seen His hand. Martha saved you.

Martha.

I am sad for her and her unholy need. She tried again under the wheels of the cart. To shake off her own life. She could have snatched Mercy away. Instead she tried again — perhaps thinking no blame, giving a life for a life. But it's no good. Her life sticks to her like dust on wet skin. Look at her walking there behind William. The rest of her clothes gone, she wears only her cotton shift again, torn now, and covers herself with the tattered remains of a tunic that falls in front like a chasuble. She walks with an even step, unfeeling. I haven't seen her stumble. Her hands hang down the way I saw them before. Submission. But Martha is made for survival, and she has no fear. Then why?

Something has happened and I don't know what it is. Some incubus is sucking away her will to live. And it isn't this danger — this is nothing to her; she has suffered as much before and yet not suffered.

In Jun-ch'eng we sat by the light of the little dish of oil with its floating wick and Martha spoke, while William was sleeping, of things unspeakable.

Jun-ch'eng was close to our new circuit. We had news of a woman there in the wild Shansi mountains. Living alone, people said. They called her *K'uang-chieh*, the Crazy Sister. We knew it was Martha. It was more than a year since she had decided to leave Lin-an for the high interior, working on her own. She had wanted to go, cried tears of happiness when she said goodbye.

Then we, too, had set out on the same route, but not by choice; no, we had to be sent by the mission office like common school teachers, away from our beautiful home in Lin-an, away from the soft and lovely countryside and into the brutal, stony cities of the North. Tsehchow, wedged in the ridge of stark mountains that cascade brokenly down to the Yellow River, China's Sorrow — Tsehchow to be ours.

We had not been there long when we heard of Martha close to us. It was curious, Martha's to be the first white

32

face we should see among those grimy northern savages. In Tsehchow we lived simply, the mission barely established. Little trouble then to leave it and make the journey to Jun-ch'eng. Chiang, the good boy, stayed behind to look after the house. We paid him, of course — and we paid our dear amah double to come with us.

Poor Lin-sao, amah to James and Edward born in Lin-an, wide and motherly as a nurse should be, and loving. But she wanted nothing to do with the foreigner in the hills. "Don't take me near that she-devil," she said. "Good luck to your Crazy Sister and you too if you go up there." I told her she had to come to protect baby Edward. Such a frail baby, his hands almost transparent. Besides, James was so little still, he would be lost without his amah. The wages convinced her; it was settled.

While William supervised, two coolies we had hired loaded the cart with clothes and food for the journey. I looked at the books we were taking as gifts; they wouldn't do at all, not for Martha. "Come on, Lin-sao," I said. "We can find something better than this." And so we rifled the trunk from Lin-an, looking for something to surprise her, to please her. There was a writing case. It was in soft red hide tooled with a design of wild flowers and had a silver inkstand engraved to match. The flowers were familiar and forgotten, flowers from home. Martha never spoke of her family and she didn't write, at least not to us, but what did it matter? The writing case was perfect.

We settled ourselves and our gifts into the cart, James wide-eyed and staring on Lin-sao's lap, Lin-sao wide-eyed and staring too, beginning to realize there was to be no turning back. William rode beside us on a little black mule and another, tied behind the cart, followed like an echo as we clattered out of the town and onto the stony west road.

Martha's village was high in the mountains. We stopped for the night in the foothills in the inn that served travellers using the pass above Jun-ch'eng. It was a great barn of a place crammed with carters and muleteers and all their freight. Every private room was taken so we joined the coolies that night in the public room, lying down with everyone else on

33

the brick k'ang. I couldn't sleep. I wondered about Martha; I knew I couldn't support the privations — was it degradation? — of work in these remote places. I knew that what I was feeling was the same apprehension the others had voiced, but I couldn't help it: Martha was not quite wise.

The next day we left the cart at the inn and formed our own mule train. James rode on William's mule, clutching the harsh tufts of mane. I followed. Lin-sao came last, sitting astride her mule with her legs in their blue cotton trousers stuck straight out and her black cloth shoes pointing to the sky. The coolies walked, one in front and one behind, the first with Edward tucked into a rush basket on his back.

We climbed all day and the September air was clear and cool under the pines. Just before noon, passing by a temple that hung on a cliff face, we rode through a wax grove. It was clear and cool in the pines. The dark trees were hung with the white wax, dripped with it so that it piled on the branches like new fallen snow. Jun-ch'eng was embedded on the side of the mountain. Houses and huts were scattered down from its walls so that the village itself was like a great boulder that had been flung onto the slope and sent splinters and fragments showering below.

She had news of our coming and was out on the road to meet us. We rounded the bend in the narrow road and there she was. Martha as she used to be — as she ought to be. Not possessed. Not inside herself. She ran towards us, laughing, waving and shouting long before we could hear what she said. Lin-sao looked alarmed and jerked her mule's head round so that William had to catch at the halter to stop her from flying back down the track. Martha came up out of breath and we climbed down from the mules and we laughed like fools and hugged, and none of us knew what the others were saying.

Martha lived in a small mud-walled house. It was reached from the village street by a narrow gate which led through a wall into a tiny courtyard. The house had only two rooms, with rush mats on the earth floor, a pale wash on the walls. In one there was a cot in the corner and a chair. Martha's trunk set under the window served as a seat, or perhaps a table.

In the other stood a table and two stools, a cupboard and a medicine chest; there was some bedding rolled against the wall near a brick hearth and one or two iron pots. There was no other furniture.

But Martha was happy. We sat in the small courtyard and drank tea while she told us about her work there. Faces looked in at the gate from time to time and vanished quickly; children peered over the wall. Martha, it seemed, was accepted — to a degree. "There's no more nastiness," she said, "no more cursing when I pass in the street, nothing of that kind. My people aren't vicious by nature, only muddled; they're innocent, you see, and the innocent are defenseless, aren't they? Against evil. They need me."

William sighed heavily. "You know, Miss Coleridge, if I were you, I'd consider this an ideal time to take some leave. You know the next revivalist conference is in Shanghai. It wouldn't hurt you to come down for that. Might do you a world of good, you know." Martha smiled. "I'm not saying you need it more than anyone else, Miss Coleridge. But we all have to re-arm." The smile detached itself. "One ought not consider oneself proof against the invasions of Satan. He can muddy anyone's thinking, you know. Even our own."

"Well, I'm afraid if he started messing around with *mine*, he'd soon be in a stew. I never was very rational at the best of times." Unable to cope with this sort of response, William looked to me for inspiration.

"Well, it's not just that," I offered. "There's your material welfare to consider."

William was encouraged. "In my opinion," he said, "living like this is no help to anyone. It's demeaning. You're at their level, Miss Coleridge."

Martha was delighted. "But exactly!" she said. "It's no good staying in one's place and trying to haul souls up: one has to get down and push from behind."

I saw William grimace, but he pressed on. He said the wattle houses were unsanitary and predicted all manner of pestilence for the foolhardy who lived in them. Martha told him to take a look in the medicine chest. "You could run the gamut of every infernal disease in this country before that chemist's shop runs out. But don't be so deadly. Isn't the house rather pretty the way it is? She ruffled the red leaves of the wild azalea invading the courtyard and said we should see it in spring.

At last William came to the point. "Miss Coleridge, it's not just the disease. Frankly — and I think it's my duty to be frank — do you think you're wise to be living alone up here?"

"Alone?" Martha clearly didn't understand. "But I have my cook. That's his room," she said, pointing to the room with the hearth. "He's moved out for you so you didn't have to stay at the inn." She was losing patience just a little. "Look, he's like a father to me. And he has a tremendous reputation with a cleaver. There can't be many villains who would want to take on Mr. Tang. You should see him kill a chicken!"

"No, I'm serious," she said finally. "Thank you for worrying but I'm safer here than if I were surrounded by all the Imperial guard."

So William did not hear what she told me that night when I woke to feed Edward and found her standing by the open door with her face to the white moon. He did not hear how when she arrived the men had spat and the women had stoned her, but then how the young men had sought her out at the inn and how one of them — always the same one — had lain on her face while the rest of them came at her, one after the other, until someone not bearing the guilt had told, and the cook had run up from the kitchens and pulled them away and how the next day, the village had seen the head of the young man, the leader, stuck in a cage on the wall, and no one had spoken against the cook when he left his job at the inn to work for the Crazy Sister setting up house in the village.

My feet will not move. Something is wrong. I feel a coldness where the baby lies. Bending slowly, my knees touch the ground. My fingers feel inside the wraps where Mercy is sleeping.

Sleeping?

My fingers feel flesh that is cool and solid. My hands run

36

over the limbs and the limbs do not move. Slowly. Slowly, I unwrap her, my baby. Her eyes are closed. Thank God her eyes are closed. Her face is gray. A tiny flake of blood has dried in the corner of her mouth.

Back and forth, back and forth, a wave cresting but not breaking, white shining against the dark night sea, a motion that lulls, that numbs. Crooning. A murmur that softens, suppresses the pain. It is Martha walking back and forth, back and forth in her white shift, picked out like a sail by the big moon, walking down there in the dry bed of the river. Singing. Keening. Whose pain?

"Yea, though I walk through the valley of the shadow of death," back and forth, "I will fear no evil," no pain. "Thy rod and Thy staff they comfort me."

Whose pain?

James? But James is sleeping, curled on the ground.

William? William is beside me. I feel his hand over mine. I hear his voice against the crooning.

"Emily? Are you awake? Shsh, don't move. I'll say the words for you."

For me? Then my pain? My loss? I feel nothing, need no words.

"She is delivered into the house of the Lord. May perpetual light shine upon her."

Mercy? No. Yes, he means Mercy. Delivered? No, no. Now I understand. I remember. I know. Now screaming, "No. No. No." Trying to make the word last forever, trying to make it take the place of all words ever, "*No* . . . "

And Martha is scrambling up the slope towards us. James sitting stark-eyed with fear in the moonlight. William and Martha keeping me still. Their hands on me make me remember. Yes, now I remember, Martha's hands holding me. Holding me away from my baby. And William bending, bending to cover my baby with stones at the foot of the hill. And then nothing.

"Thy kingdom come. Thy will be done."

"*Stop!*" Scream at them, "Stop! How can you pray to Him?

37

He's forgotten us. Our God has forsaken us!" They're trying to stop me but nothing can stop me. I *shall* speak the truth. "Mercy lived. She was living. I felt her, warm, alive on me, living. And then nothing. He forgot. Forgot to keep her alive. We're nothing to Him. Less than ants that crawl over the earth. *He has forsaken us.*"

William is turning his head away. Is he crying for Mercy? For us all? For God? But Martha is speaking. She cradles James. Words are pouring from her, songs of love and forgiveness, visions of hope, prophesies, promises.

Poison.

The words a stream that is poison in my soul. Stop my ears. Stop my mouth. Lie still. Let them believe I drink the poisoned words. Drink the lies.

Quiet now. Lay my head here in William's lap. Shut my mind to his prayers for forgiveness. Make my own words to God. To their God. Oh Lord, I have questioned Your goodness, Your divine wisdom. Oh Lord, I have borne my cross with anger. Yes Lord, I have despaired. And still I question and still I rage and yes, Lord, I do despair and I do not repent.

But you, William. Meek like a lamb. Like a dog. Taking the stick that has beaten its back and nervously, cravenly licking it. William. Time was when you raged. Remember that wave of cholera in filthy Tsehchow? You showed your anger then. You raged, William, straight in the face of your God and you'd have nothing to do with acceptance until long after the little one, Edward, was gone. And then, when you were quiet and had taught yourself it had to be, even then you didn't repent but only told to your God, simply, without apology, how it was you came to speak the angry words.

Such a long night and the moon still staring down as if it cannot look long enough on the pile of stones at the foot of the hill. William is trying to sleep. He opens his mouth again and again making a hollow sound. Perhaps he is thinking of water. His lips pull apart slowly. The skin stretches and lets go.

38

The shame of those prayers that came from his lips. Nothing but insurance for his own soul, precautionary measures, "Almighty God, she does not know what she is saying, my dear wife, be merciful to her — and to me. Please."

It sickens me but I know I should feel pity. He doubts his own position; the ground he stands on is rocking under him. What I see, what I hear from him is a mask and a borrowed voice; he has lost himself. Where? When? He had faith. Yes he had. Now he has only words.

My own words are like echoes. I have asked the questions before. I have seen the mask on another face: Martha's. The same piety put on for me? No. Nor for themselves. For each other then. Both of them skilled in its use: the sticky words, the false humility, the idiot submission. Why? William may be scrabbling for his drowning soul, but Martha? She would damn her soul to be rid of her life and yet she spewed out a stream of visions and promises. Both of them, William and Martha, are wrapping me round, cocooning us all with a web of hypocrisy. Now. At this time of all times. What can be the use of bartering with God?

It's a simple matter of survival: animal strength and human wit and nothing else. And Martha has them.

I hate her.

Look at her now. Her face calm and quiet, her mouth composed, almost smiling. She isn't dreaming, like William, of water that doesn't exist.

Try now to sleep.

The boats at Auldbury had been long out of use. Their wood was damp and soft where the paint had come off and slicked over in places with green. Not exactly seaworthy but they would do for the Mourne. We could row up to Archer's Lake. Hardly a lake at all. Once a bend in the river, now it lay back behind the long grasses, a quiet crescent of light cut in the marshy green.

The boats bumped softly against the bank while we settled ourselves.

Mother removed her new straw hat and fluffed at the brim

39

irritably. "It's no use, I'll have to change. I shall be caught up in the willows with this ridiculous brim."

"Mother, your old straw is just as — wide." But Mother was already demanding Frederick's hand to help her out of the skiff and she sauntered with her lazy walk back to the house.

So we waited, Frederick and Dora in the skiff, silent, a tartan rug spread for Mother over the seat in the stern, William and Florence and I in the longer boat, the gondola we called it, talking of nothing. Grandfather watched with Dora's children from the bank. Poor old Grandfather, a feeble substitute for Father, hauled out of his Cape Breton lair for the week so that William could make his request.

The entire week was orchestrated around that single interview. For William, nothing else mattered. The dinner parties, the pleasure jaunts, the luncheons were nothing but distractions from his purpose.

I was sorry for William. He was so out of place, but he made matters worse; there was something that he lacked — tolerance, patience? I couldn't name it then. He could scarcely hide his eagerness to be gone. His restraint was a dam and a huge reservoir of energy was building behind it. The China mission and our marriage were inextricably linked — and he was impatient for them both.

We watched Mother coming back. She stopped at the bench to speak with Grandfather, saying everything twice to his vacant eyes, then she came down the bank and unhurriedly, gracefully, picked up her skirts and finally stepped into the skiff. Almost immediately she stepped out again with a great deal of head shaking. She held on to Frederick while she made a pantomime of examining her shoes.

"No. This is impossible. They'll be soiled terribly. Look at the water in there. Her bottom is out. It must be."

"It's only rainwater, Mrs. Fisk. Don't worry."

"No, I'm sorry. I shall not sit with my feet in the river. Not at any cost."

I looked at William. His expression was carefully neutral. I offered to exchange places with Mother but she was calling

40

to Grandfather to go to the house to ask Mrs. Gale for a basin to bail out the skiff.

At this Dora stirred herself from where she had sat unmoved in the bow. "Mother, please. Grandfather mustn't leave the children."

"Oh, Dora, don't fuss. They'll be perfectly all right. Now look. He's on his way back to see what you want. We could have had the basin by now."

"Mother, we really don't need a basin." I tried to make my offer heard again, "Please take my place in the gondola. It's perfectly dry."

William had not changed his pose of polite readiness for the silly excursion, but I saw his exasperation. Florence continued to arrange the cushions. Frederick asked leave to light a cigar with all the impudent, pretended innocence of a visitor to a gunpowder works. In due course we were all seated again and we cast off, Frederick taking the skiff with Dora and me, William striking out into the stream with Mother and Florence — and the cushions — in the long, narrow boat.

They reached the weir at the lake long before us and were waiting there when our skiff swung in against the bank. We climbed out and stood in the wet grass. We watched the men, William in his shirt sleeves, Frederick closing one eye against the smoke of his cigar, pull the boats up out of the stream and across into the lake. William, even with Mother to contend with, had his party embarked and his boat underway long before Frederick had started. I watched him rowing fiercely out there on the little lake thick with weeds, caught in a backwater as Father had been. *Let him go to China*, I thought, *and let me be with him.*

I turned back to watch Frederick. The blades of his oars dipped into the murky water, pulled and let go their resistance, slipping up into the air before the stroke was complete. There was something curiously annoying about the imperfection of it. I thought I understood, as well as if it were my own, William's need for action.

We made out into the middle of the lake where the sun was shining, brightening the water. Frederick stopped rowing and rested the oars. Dora sighed and closed her eyes. The boat rocked gently like a cradle, inviting rest, persuading me to let go.

"Ah, ladies," said Frederick, "isn't this a perfect day to be cut adrift?"

It is cold and the stones at the foot of the hill will be cold.

I am stiff and bruised. James is pressing against me, searching for warmth. Cold. Then no clouds building. Another day of drought. We cannot stay here on the hill without water. But the riverbed will be like a trough catching the sun's rays. We should leave before the sun begins to climb. Before the sun warms the stones.

Cold. And the rocks wet? I stretch my hand behind my head. I touch a hard, damp surface. James sits up sleepily and watches without speaking as I crawl to the rock and run my tongue over its surface. It soothes. It moistens. I wipe my hand over the wet rock and pass it across James's nose and mouth. He is with me. We lick the rock. I wake the others and they do the same.

William gives thanks.

The light is spreading fast but we move slowly. Our limbs are stiff and sore from the trials of yesterday. We have bound our feet again, William and James and I. It will take until nightfall to reach Hsiang-ch'eng.

At the foot of the hill we stop. We stand before the pile of stones and bow our heads. James gathers some more small ones and makes a cross with them on the ground. I only look. I think how, when the rain comes, their colors, tawny and pink, will shine in the wetness.

We follow Martha as she turns and begins to walk.

The road still runs beside the riverbed. Sometimes it disappears completely in places where the river once broke its banks and washed it away, scouring out its mark with rocks and boulders. Then we walk in the riverbed. Such a volume of water to move the land. Today not even a stain. The yellow silt is caked into a smooth crust. It is cracked like the glaze on old porcelain. At first today we left prints behind as our feet broke the crust. Now we make no impression. The earth has buried the water. It is sealing it in.

Poor James. He walks with Martha, holding her hand, trying to match her long step. The rags bound on his feet make him stumble often. He'll be exhausted before the morning has passed. And yet he welcomes each day, even now, smiling when he finds himself awake in the world. He still hasn't learned to look forward. Or back. He lives his life in a nest of Chinese boxes, each day a separate box. As he passes from one to the next, the door closes behind him. It shuts on the pain of yesterday; he finds himself whole again. Until the next blow, the next escape, the next door. And no box gives him any clue to the contents of the one to come.

But the boxes are numbered. Soon the puzzle will be finished and he will know. He will be cursed with knowing, like the rest of us. He will see that we walk on a road and there are no doors to stop us from looking back at the figures we leave behind, at the small piles of stones that are all that remain.

And we know too what lies ahead. Look at the three of us walking, William and I grieving for yesterday, fearing today, Martha disdaining grief and fear both. Martha desiring only an end to it.

Look at the three of us stripped of our faith, our eyes stuck open. Nowhere to look but at ourselves. And the truth as loud as the brassy sun overhead.

Faith. I call it faith but I wonder. It was no gift from God, it was a tool of our own making. And weren't we intent there in Shanghai, forging, tempering, battering it into shape? For two whole years. To come away with what? A weapon stamped with the imprimatur of heaven? Something to lay low all opposition.

We believed at last that we had arrived: Shanghai — the great carved door to the temple of China. We believed we were in touch with the teeming millions. The flood of souls. We believed.

Oh, the signs were there to convince us. Filth and squalor everywhere, just what we had come for, the very air sopping with the nauseous smells. The stench of it all seeped even into the settlement. And the noise. The walls rang with it — the braying, squawking, creaking, grinding din.

And the people. Oh, yes, teeming millions, certainly — all crammed at once inside that city's walls, babbling, trading, quarrelling. We saw it all; we smelled it and we heard it and we thought we were touching China. We weren't even close. We smelled the incense and did not know the prayer, saw the disease and couldn't feel the pain. Chloroformed by our own exaltation. Sweet excitement.

True sinophiles, I wrote to Dora. *We're becoming true sinophiles. Can't you just see William when he shaves his head and wears a queue?* But of course you never did, did you William? It was a game and we could bend whatever rules we wanted. We set the rules, after all — and the consulate kept them for us. I can hear Dr. Willis's voice now: "The diplomatic staff — there's your key. If you want to open those inner doors the diplomatic staff's the key." And we used it. But did you really see the diplomatic circle as an opening? It was a stockade, William. With its gunboats and telegraphs, its statements and its bluster it was a stockade against the people.

Even our servants, culled, washed and top-and-tailed by the starched and ruffled Mrs. Willis, they weren't the real China. They were hand-picked men and women who could launder for us, cook for us, clean for us and wait on us in flawless mimicry of our taste. Trained monkeys. And Christian converts all, weren't they, William? But even that wasn't enough for you. I remember you making them sign the pledge, each male servant, to renounce concubinage — forever.

Doesn't the memory sting you now?

Sinophiles. Nothing could be further from the truth. We wanted only to fashion them in our own image, these unlikely teeming, seething, coupling millions. Oh, yes, a vast undertaking, but we were equal to it weren't we? We never questioned that.

It was Dr. Willis who took us on our first tour of the city.

"We'll just take ourselves up here," he said, pointing to one of the walls with steps leading up to the top. "Marvellous view. You'll see practically the whole of the native market from here." Martha struck out towards the main press of people. "I think you'd do well to stay with the party," Dr. Willis said, as if there were no question of her doing otherwise.

Martha didn't listen.

We looked out across the awnings and the smoke from the cooking fires and watched the buying and the selling, the bartering and begging and thieving. There was a group of ragged men moving from stall to stall. The vendors would throw them one or two cash. The men fought over the coins. "Extortionists," said Dr. Willis. "They threaten violence if they don't get their money. It's all a racket." And there was an ancient woman, with a tiny child on her back, who also stopped at every stall. "For sale," said Dr. Willis. It took me a while to realize that he meant the child. I wanted to find out more but a large cart rolled by, noisily close to us. It was piled so high with bales of cotton that it looked as if it would tip on a slight turn. A young boy, a child not more than ten, shared the traces with a mule.

"I think I've seen all I want to see for now, thank you." My voice seemed to be coming from somewhere outside of me.

We turned then and walked back along the wall, but when we reached the head of the stairs Dr. Willis said that the way was blocked. We retraced our steps and found a way down further along. "But you'll want to see what that was all about," said Dr. Willis.

Walking back along the base of the wall, we came to the stairs we had first taken. There at the foot someone had dragged into place a great cage of heavy bamboo. Inside was a man. The cage seemed to have been built around him; it ended high at his neck, so that his head stuck out at an unnatural angle, as if it were on a plate.

"Common criminal," said Dr. Willis and flipped the bill that was tacked to the front of the cage. "It doesn't say any more."

The man inside stared blankly ahead. No one else bothered even to look at him. "These are your people," I whispered to

45

William on our way across the city. "They're yours, and they're waiting for you." I praised God for every hungry belly and parched throat, not wanting to think about the cruelty of man — or of God. It was years, it was all these seven long wasted years before I could do that.

"And this is our pride and joy." Dr. Willis expanded visibly with his smile. "We've been busy every day since we opened."

The clinic was in one of the poorer quarters. The door on the street opened to a large waiting room. Most of the patients were seen and treated right there where they sat or lay. To one side was a surgery reserved for the most critical cases. It was full. At the back the chronically sick were isolated in a few whitewashed rooms surrounding a small compound. Beside each cot was a Bible.

Without warning, as we stood numbly in the silence, a sudden noise of shouting and scuffling broke from the waiting room. Men were pulling someone in and there was blood everywhere. We stood back to let Dr. Willis through and then I saw. The man on the floor was an opium addict, they said, and had tried to kill himself. The strange, bubbling tear in his throat was made by the wire he had tightened with his own hands.

In our extremity now, how well I understand what moved those crippled bodies and made the twisted fingers clutch at the Bible in their pain. I see now the blank eyes that fixed only on survival while we scrutinized them closely for evidence of conversion. And the lips, dry and parched, that promised "Yes." Yes I will. I believe. I do believe. Only stop the pain.

I understand. And when the time comes I will do the same. My lips will lie for release. My lips will recant, denounce, forswear. Anything. Only let us survive. Let us live.

But I must put down this fear, this hydra. Cling to hope. We have time yet. In Hsiang-ch'eng we'll find help. They'll know our rights there. Just get there. Get there. In Hsiang-ch'eng it will be just like Lin-an. We'll be protected, secure. It's only here in the moldering heart of the country that the rebels have taken hold. They can't have gone further. It can't

46

be like this across the border. It can't. Surely.

William's hand is on mine. He pulls gently. "Only a little further, Emily. Then we can rest. Look, Martha's waiting with James."

There is no shade. They've stopped in the road. Martha squats, her knees wide apart and little James standing between them. He leans against her, rests his forehead against hers. They do not look up as we come to them. William has his arms around my shoulders. He's trying to make me sit down, handling me as if I were a lunatic.

I shake him off and go to them. I see that James's skin on his arms and neck is red, seared with the sun. The little face. I turn it up to mine. His eyes are wide and unhappy, staring at me above his blistered nose. His lips are swollen and cracked and he holds them slightly apart but he doesn't speak. Oh, James! Eyes barely human; an animal in pain, submitting to the heat.

But not succumbing. Not yet. I rest his head gently back against Martha. She smiles slightly under her closed eyes. I sit down behind her and we let our backs close together until their weight is equalized. I put out my hand to William. "We must pray, Emily," he says, then kneels a little distance off and joins his hands. I think his shoulders are shaking — or is it the haze?

I close my eyes.

Lin-an. Yes — think of Lin-an. James's birthplace ... and Edward's. Where our lives were whole; everything working to its rightful end. City of warm stone. Bricks pink in the dawn. Rain dripping from roofs, the tiles shining green and gold. Courtyards swept and washed in the early morning. Colored quilts hanging from the open windows. Pigeons flying up from the curved eaves. The duck pond in the compound where yellow-footed ducks paddled, plump and white. The grassy moat outside the walls where the boys played and swam. The green hills swelling softly behind the city and the bamboo groves where the sun flashed through the striped shade as we walked.

47

We were in Toronto, on furlough, when we first heard of Lin-an. The Pritchards had been writing regularly to mission headquarters since their arrival in China — sad, bleating letters:

> We fear we shall not be able to retain the property in the face of opposition.

> Mrs. Pritchard's health worsens visibly.

> Today our faithful dog was killed when ruffians stormed the compound.

> We are of no use, either to the people or to the Lord above.

And always there were the words that remained unwritten: Call us home.

William despised their weakness but he found the charity to keep silent in that matter. We applied for the post, the committee approved, and I wrote to Martha. She was still in Shanghai at the time, afraid to leave its glorious chaos for a moment, as if the Yangtze might suddenly rise and swallow it up. *Be ready to leave on our return,* I wrote. *We've found the perfect situation.*

In Shanghai Martha had settled everything. William had only to supervise the loading of the trunks aboard the *Bodekin* for Hangchow. We took with us two servants. Martha had tried to dismiss her houseboy, Ts'ai, but he worked himself into an astonishing state of woe, wept a few real tears and said if she left without him he'd spend his final wages on a cord to hang himself. "Not without dropping in at the opium den first," said Martha quietly. "He'll never remember to hang himself after that." She relented, nevertheless.

And then there was Chiang. William hired him the day before we sailed. Chiang shed a few tears of his own when he found out what was in the contract he signed. So reluctant was he to go that William paid a coolie to watch him all through the night while the *Bodekin* lay at anchor. Next morning he came to us, beaming across his broken teeth where the coolie had hit him. He pledged his loyalty in quaintly medieval terms — for the length of his days.

Poor Chiang. If he had known. We took him further than Lin-an, made him everything from valet to muleteer. And now perhaps martyr, with no one to bury him in wild Tsehchow. Poor Chiang. If only he had listened to his heart when the *Bodekin*'s paddle shook her frame and she turned for Hangchow.

In Hangchow we rested (Martha was restless but we persuaded her to stay) — one week of pale sun and curling mists drifting across the lake. We walked in temple gardens where the orange silk of the priests' robes whispered between the colonnades; we sat in marble pavilions and watched the shadow of the hills spread across the water; and just before sunset we rode out in rickshaws to watch the pagoda roofs turn red and gold before we raced back towards the flickering torches that showed the gates still open.

The city's beauty was cool and serene: white and green, marble and willow, mists lifting to show blue hills, and clear water springing from jade fountains. Reflections of its carved halls trembled and stilled as the boats slid by. White doves vanished with a soft rush beneath the sea-green tiles of its eaves.

We left in the early morning, shuddering awake in the freshness, watching the city slip away as our houseboat made upstream. Although the river was easy, we made slow progress. William paid a fair daily rate and the men rewarded him whenever they could by letting down the sail and drifting into the bank. They said the wind was wrong, or the tides, or the dragon god. If there were rapids, or rocks, they waited for a lucky day. Sometimes they tracked, harnessing themselves like animals to the bamboo pole and dragging the boat along beside the bank. But there was always delay; then they would stop and offer some muddled excuse and sit down on the bank to smoke and play their endless gambling games.

Martha watched them sometimes from the walkway as they tracked. When they rested she stared at them from the entrance

49

of our living quarters. It offended William. "Miss Coleridge, come inside," he said. "You'll be offended there."

But Martha didn't take her eyes from the glistening backs hunched over the dice. "Their lives are so bestial. We have to help."

The next evening, when they rested, Martha went to the boatmen as they crouched round their fire. They had been telling bawdy stories, their laughter coarse and disturbing. Martha tried to talk with them but they only stared at her in bemused silence and waited until she had gone inside, when they began again, louder than before.

When we reached Fuyang, William said it was just as well that we had finished with the river. We made arrangements to leave immediately for Lin-an by cart, with the rest of the baggage to follow when the little cargo boat arrived. Farmers rested on their hoes to watch us pass, but as we drew near to Lin-an the people's interest in us grew less and less placid; some of them began to jeer and spit; one or two picked up stones. Ts'ai scrambled to the bottom of the cart and stayed there.

At the city, a crowd of idlers had grouped themselves defensively in the gateway. Chiang ran ahead, waving his arms and shouting, "Make way! Make way!"

And when the crowd began to close on him, William didn't hesitate. He stood up in the cart and bellowed: "Let the foreign devils pass."

At the magistrate's district office, the yamen, William demanded and received an immediate audience. He reminded the official of the freedom of foreign missionaries, sanctioned by the Imperial court, to travel and reside wherever we wished, without molestation; he hinted at our just recourse to the consul at Tientsin should we remain unsatisfied. The district magistrate, by definition a political man, understood at once what was required; William came away with the magistrate's official card, safe lodgings, an escort, and a promise of retribution for the incident at the gate.

It was easy then. Hardly a conflict at all. Something drove us through all the obstacles. Faith or blindness? Look at William here. Kneeling, bowed, cowed. Begging to the empty sky. Not Martha. She is as strong now as she was then. She never shows fear, never. I used to think she was blind to hardship and risk. Now I know she seeks them out — her greatest needs. Well, she has them now. Here on this God-empty plain, under the sting of the sun.

And still she is yearning.

William gets up and comes to us. Martha looks up as he touches her shoulder. "Yes, William, you're right. We'd better move on before we seize up completely."

James tries to burrow deeper against her as she moves. He kicks and then gives up as William goes to take him. His lips are so blistered I don't think he can speak.

"Here. Let me take him for a while." Martha asking for a cross to bear, as if what we have isn't enough.

William manages to get James onto her back and we walk again. More slowly now. We walk behind Martha. William holding me behind the elbow as if I might fall. I tell him that I feel all right but it isn't true. My insides are racked and twisted. These are convulsions I recognize: dysentery. The plague of this filthy country. If one is strong enough to survive the cholera, the typhus and all the rest, there is still dysentery. This humiliating visitation that weakens us, slowly, continually. I feel a drawing, dragging sensation in my limbs. I must have water, clean water soon to purge this foulness.

Soon. Force the mind away from the thought of water. Like trying not to touch a sore. Keep a stranglehold on thought. Watch the ground roll back under my step, my feet grotesque in their rags. Watch Martha's feet. The toes spread at each step under the weight of her extra burden. I watch to see them flinch at the sharpness of the stones. They do not. Insensible. The step is measured, flat, springless. The tread of a mystic, a firewalker.

Remember Martha in the bamboo groves behind Lin-an. See her setting out for the villages around the city from the very first day with her bag of plasters and salves and her tracts. The

51

vigor still in her step when she returned, brimming. She needed work, her life's blood. Nothing in moderation. William, waiting for the full supplies to arrive before he opened the dispensary, would send Ts'ai out after her. But Ts'ai balked, saying the city ruffians were too much for him. Yet Martha always returned, fresh and smiling, her innocence her talisman — an innocence so terrible it began to look like courage. A foreign devil, a foreign she-devil, walking abroad, unaccompanied, unafraid. She terrified the people — and she was safe.

It was too much for Ts'ai. He cut himself off from his eccentric mistress and, perhaps thinking it might be safer to be on their side, took up with the very youths who had terrorized him. For a while Martha paid him his wages whenever she could find him but the money fed only his appetite for opium and he was dead, starved, within the year.

But the difficulties were nothing then. To William any sign of hostility was just another nuisance — like the flies or the language — that had somehow or other to be got out of the way. He had his arrogance, his conviction to carry us over; and, yes, I had faith in William. I had William, I had my Bible and in time I had my babies, James, growing fat and happy with our fat and happy amah, and then Edward.

And the people not long to come over to us. At first, they came out of curiosity and bravado, and then they came out of need. The surgery was their purgatory; afraid to go there they nevertheless steeled themselves to it and came away marvellously, magically cleansed — of all their minor ailments, at least. And what reason had they to question our motives? They had difficulties enough without closing the door on a new prospect of celestial assistance — whether from a stranger God or their own.

The Sunday congregation at the hall that served for a church with its blackened roof-beams and earthen floor increased steadily.

But Martha was restless. She began to spend more and more of her time in the outlying villages — and then on an impulse she left. It was in March when we had the party from Foochow staying with us: the Coopers, who were to remain, and the Gordons, who were on their way to the interior. March in Lin-an. The sky washed in the changing brightnesses, high as the pale moon. The air blown with promises of blossom, freaked with the cries of birds gathering to fly north.

One morning Martha came in to breakfast, kissed us both and said that she would be leaving with the Gordons. The next day she was gone. I felt as if our lives were becalmed.

The Coopers stayed on. An energetic couple who tugged at and harried the people like a pair of wiry terriers until they had them not only in the surgery and the church but at their opium clinics and their reading class and their hymn practice, too. "To improve upon the dreadful din we — and the good Lord also — must bear each week." And then they, too, left — or, at least, Dr. Cooper left. His wife remained, buried within the walls of the compound, all her practical common sense, all his medical expertise come to nothing against the cholera. STRICKEN IN THE MIDST OF HER GLORIOUS WORK read the great stone slab over her grave.

Then William and I alone there in those months. After dinner Lin-sao would take care of James and Chiang would be busy in the kitchen. We would sit out on the low, stone seat in the compound and watch the ducks, pale forms in the dusky light, settling against the sandy earth, their movements reminding me of the baby turning, settling inside me. We would sit on and watch the twisted pattern of the magnolia branches against the thickening dark, and wait for the hour for bed. The mission was ours. We had everything we had asked for from China.

One night lying awake, listening to the splay-footed frogs that clung to the stone walls and waiting for the first sounds from the geese so that I could get up and watch the dawn seep over the city walls, I looked at William's dark head on the pillow. He lay face down, one arm reaching up and bent around the pillow. A memory of an embrace. I thought of us together. Our longing for each other like a sickness, an addiction, and no respite ever. William burned with guilt; but in the mornings, as I prayed beside him, asking forgiveness for our lack of restraint, I felt only the sweetness of the remembered touch.

I got up quietly and went to sit by the open window. There I wrote to Dora and tried to tell her. How we had found our heaven. How I felt conscience-stricken for wanting no other.

This land has the beauty of life itself, I wrote. *China is our mother. She gives us the fruits of the earth, the sweet rain, the love of the people.*

But, of course, none of it was true. We were *in* China but not *of* her. We lived inside a glass bubble. Masses thronged outside the glass but didn't break it. We viewed the outside with a clarity that was convincing but we heard no protests or cries, smelled no corruption; neither did we taste any bitter gall nor ache with any pain. In our glass bubble we floated, circling each other in an endless dance, mirroring ourselves.

There was a pool in the temple gardens in Hangchow. There the monks kept fish for the simple pleasure of their movement: great carp that slid low on the muddy bottom, shubunkins that lifted to the surface to kiss the air with their thick lips. In the centre was a glass bowl. In the bowl two black fish. They bore their young live and so were kept apart for the protection of their kind. The two black fish circled the bowl again and again. The female was full-bellied and from time to time convulsed to drop a tiny black inkspot of fish. The arrival of her time aroused the male that sometimes tried to couple with her as she swam. And all the while, in the outer pool, the carp and the catfish nosed in the sludge and the minnows dashed their blunt faces against the glass in their efforts to reach the fry.

Part Two

September 1899, Tsehchow

Just above the steep drop down into Tsehchow the mule track broke free of the dark pines. The travellers, three riders and two coolies on foot, came out in single file, casting long shadows in front of them into the thin sunlight. The light fell first on the coolie who ran ahead. He was ragged but clean-skinned and the only load he carried was a rush basket on his back. He kept his head down, watching for loose rocks or roots across the track. As he ran he breathed noisily, blowing out his lungfuls of air a little at a time at every step until the next giant inhalation. His run was no faster than a dogtrot and his feet scuffed the loose track as he went but he kept his knees well bent and his weight low so that there was no shock to the upper part of his body, only a slight, easy shift from side to side.

The baby in the rush basket slept, deep in its quilted wrap. Behind the coolie rode a white man with a small boy. The man was tall and angular. He wore a Chinese gown of black silk but it pulled across his shoulders like a shirt on a chair back and its hem rested high on his calves over the dark gray cloth of his trousers. His black hair was cut to the neck of his gown and he kept the long strands brushed back but he did not tie them. While his pale blue eyes stared ahead vacantly his arms hugged the little boy in front of him and moved protectively to keep him balanced. The child himself, not more than four, clutched at the mule's harsh mane and blinked with exaggeration whenever she faltered, as if that might help him stay on.

The man stopped and turned, resting one hand on the mule's rump while he waited for the young woman who followed. He was pleased to see that the innkeeper had been right and that the track had brought them out, as he said it would, just above Tsehchow. It soothed his anger over the theft of the cart. The innkeeper, floundering in the depths of his apologies, pouring out lamentations for the dishonor that had fallen on his house, said it had been stolen one night while they were up at Jun-ch'eng. But of course the man was lying, thought William. He strongly suspected that the cart had been sold the moment they left the inn for Martha's village. What a fool he'd been to trust the man. Someone would have to pay.

In fact, the more he thought about it, the more he realized this was just the kind of disrespect for foreigners that was becoming far too common. Flagrant breaches of treaty rights. Wouldn't do a bit of good to let the matter drop; next poor soul who happened along would be cheated out of the shirt off his back.

William decided to see the district magistrate at Tsehchow first thing in the morning.

The young woman rode out of the shadow. She sat very straight astride a wild looking mule and jerked hard on the reins whenever it plunged its head down. She was small and slim and wore a padded Chinese jacket and trousers. Seen from a distance only her hair betrayed her. It hung down heavily over one shoulder in a thick, flamboyant auburn braid. Her face was pale, almost like linen except where shadows purpled the skin round her eyes. She smiled at the man but her smile said nothing; her thoughts were elsewhere.

She was followed closely by a Chinese servant, a much older woman, round and chunky, riding a docile, willing mare with all the ease and nonchalance of someone sitting on a tiger. Her feet, in their black cotton slippers, stuck straight up to the blue sky.

The riders went on in close file. Behind them ran the second coolie carrying the rest of the baggage, wrapped in oilcloth and tied in two huge bundles to the pole across his shoulders. He chanted softly to himself. Sometimes he broke the rhythm of his chant and gurgled a lewd phrase for the pleasure of seeing Lin-sao's black-slippered feet go rigid with indignation. Then his lips would slide apart in a gummy smile and he would take up his chant again.

His voice was lost on William and Emily. They rode without speaking, neither noticing the other's silence, both thinking of Martha, wild, vulnerable; the Crazy Sister spinning out her soul like a kite in the high mountain air. No one had told William what had happened, but the few words he had overheard as the two women stood talking in the moonlight were enough. He added them to the gleanings of his conversation with Tang and he came close to the truth.

Tang, Martha's Mr. Tang, had drawn William aside soon after their arrival and begged him to take Martha back with them before it was too late. "T'ai-t'ai not must stay at Jun-ch'eng more," he had said, and the broken words had sounded desperately serious.

"And why not?"

"One time badness have come. More badness have come by and by."

"What do you mean, *badness*?"

"Tang not speak more. If T'ai-t'ai stay, T'ai-t'ai catch more badness by and by. T'ai-t'ai have no master. Tang not speak more. Master know. Master listen master heart and hear Tang."

And William had known in his heart what had happened — what *must* have happened — to Martha alone in that remote village. She couldn't stay now. Yet she had thwarted every argument of his, not knowing that he knew. Or perhaps knowing, after all. In any event, he couldn't persuade her to leave. The magistrate again? Take the matter up with him? Impossible. There were too many false allegations against the mission as it was. The matter could never go to the district court. The victim was as guilty as the criminal there and it wouldn't do the cause any good at all, besides putting Martha in serious danger. The consulate then? William dismissed that too since it must involve the magistrate. He thought of the mission itself. He could arrange for Central Office to call her home on some pretext — any pretext. The mission mustn't know what had happened. He remembered his arguments on Martha's behalf during the recruiting; *the mission must never know* . . . On grounds of health then? But Martha was as strong as a coolie and had never suffered a day's sickness. The woman would refuse.

William tried to compose in his head a letter to Central Office stating the bald truth. Which was? . . . He admitted to himself that he really didn't know. His mind held only images of indescribable filth when he tried to articulate what had — what *probably* had — occurred. It was pointless to pursue this train of thought. Suppose he were to broach the matter with Toronto; suppose they were to respond with a compulsory furlough: it wouldn't make any difference to Martha. She had cut herself loose and, with or without their blessing, Martha, he knew, would stay.

Reluctantly, William began to accept the responsibility of knowledge. To pass on this knowledge to a third party would be to shelve his own responsibility to act, and it could only damage Martha. He had to go back soon, and he had to make her come away. He could not stop thinking about Emily in Martha's place.

Emily smiled at him abstractedly as he turned to look at her. She was still with Martha. On their last night there, Emily got up again in the quiet hours, knowing she would find Martha again at the open door, staring at the white moon. She had pleaded with her to return with them to Tsehchow.

"You'll die here, Martha. You can't survive a thing like that."

"But I have survived. Pinch me."

"Be serious, Martha. You can't stay."

"I am serious. And I'm staying."

"And if it happens again? You're putting yourself at risk, and if it *does* happen again, Martha, you'll share the guilt, you know that. If you live."

"Do you really believe that? You take the guilt along with the blow when you turn the other cheek? Is that what it's all about?"

"That's not the same. Putting yourself in the way of temptation for others is another matter altogether."

"In that case, my dear, you'd better run home and lock yourself away until you wither and shrivel and that wicked red hair drops out in gray shreds."

Emily had smiled — but not warmly — and without another word had gone back in to sleep.

They had said little at parting but now, riding farther and

60

farther from the village, leaving Martha there at risk again, Emily was uneasy. Her conscience prickled like a numbed limb coming back to life. She should have tried again to make Martha leave. She couldn't understand her not wanting to run from the place. But then that would change nothing. The foulness and the impurity would be with Martha always. She would never feel clean again. It occurred to Emily that that might be Martha's reason for staying. Perhaps she never could leave now, never return to society. Was the victim as guilty as the criminal? She'd said almost as much.

"*Wang yu-pien tsou!*" The hoarse voice of the coolie guide croaked out the orders to turn for the descent into Tsehchow. The track was scarcely visible and the mules picked their own paths down the steep, bare slope, their hooves clicking against the stones and their rumps pitching and rolling as their legs worked against the gradient.

Emily tried to hurry her argument to its conclusion, like a sleeper trying to finish a dream before waking. It seemed hard to believe, and yet if she were to stay and expose herself to more sin, then surely there must be guilt. Guilt — or else perfect, spotless innocence. Martha a saint? The question irritated Emily. She plumped for guilt and began to concentrate on the descent. Turning, she looked to see how Lin-sao was faring behind her. The poor amah's legs were tucked back now like chicken wings as her upper body strained back away from the mule's dipping neck. Emily smiled broadly and called encouragement.

"Your mule has good feet. Trust her. She won't let you fall."

At this, Lin-sao's eyes widened in terror and then closed tightly. Emily waited and caught at the mule's headpiece as it drew level.

The amah's eyes were still closed.

"See, Lin-sao? Isn't it beautiful?"

Hardly moving her head, Lin-sao opened her eyes and followed Emily's pointing finger. Tsehchow was spread below them like a wasp's nest broken open in the sun. The north-south road was the line of the break. There were the fragments, the houses outside the walls and there, the buildings, streets and alleys, the thousand connected cells.

Lin-sao smiled. The two women scanned the north road until they found the tiny flecks of camels moving (but barely, it seemed), on their long journey back to Peking. The southbound mules returning to Hankow were too distant to be seen but they would be there on the road, part of the endless cycle of silk for pottery for tea for iron for rice, the eternal exchange of riches that passed in and out of the cities.

The amah relaxed and followed Emily's mule down.

On the road William gave instructions for everyone to stay close together. He had no fears for the safety of any of them; the consequences of tampering with a foreigner were thoroughly promulgated and understood. He feared perhaps least of all for Edward, bobbing along, snug on the back of his coolie; but their baggage, he thought nervously, could be conveniently lost in the crowds. William positioned the second carrier well in front.

As they approached the walls, which glowed steadily gold in the low rays of the sun, the noise of the city trapped within boomed indistinctly. Nearer, familiar features, signatures, began to separate from the mass of sound until, as the travellers passed through the second set of gates, the whole body of noise exploded about them in a riot of discord. The streets were jammed with people and carts, merchandise and animals.

William was annoyed to find Emily and Lin-sao parted from him almost immediately. While they were unlikely to be harmed they were certain to attract attention — a foreign devil always did. William concentrated on the men in front of him threading their way through the streets.

As for Emily, it was all she could do to keep control of her ill-tempered mule as they passed through the market quarter. She had no time to look for William. The mule swung its head wildly at sudden noises and kicked and snapped at every other beast, drawing attention to Emily on every side. "*Yang kuei tze!*" Foreign devil! The familiar insult was screeched after her but the press of traffic and confusion of movement kept her at one remove from further attention until the mule, wheeling suddenly to snatch at a bale of straw, backed into a barber as he bent over his customer's shining head. Passersby roared with delight.

Up in a moment and shouting angrily, the men were trying to grab at Emily and the mule when Lin-sao, stocky and determined, pushed in front of them. She blocked their path with her own mount, allowing time for the crowd to close again behind Emily, then she turned her own mule's head to follow, leaving the men spitting and hurling abuse at her broad back.

Alone now among her countrymen, Lin-sao began to feel conspicuous and foolish. An amah mounted on a mule. She climbed down and led the beast, weaving through the maze of streets to the compound. She breathed a sigh of relief when Chiang opened the gates for her. He grinned hugely as she stuffed the reins into his hands.

In the days that followed, William spent a great deal of time at the yamen. There was the matter of the cart. Without this extra business to settle with the magistrate, he might have returned for Martha straight away, but he found it difficult to resist such an early opportunity to establish his standing in the city once and for all. Because the cart had disappeared at the inn, in the foothills outside the city, William pressed his case home with more than his usual confidence; there would be no townsman to harbor a grudge against him if he should win the suit, only an innkeeper a day's ride away.

Resting the case on the threat of consular action, William won this suit, but it took several days to negotiate a just punishment for the innkeeper and fair recompense for himself. He settled at last for a new cart and damages for the cost of the coolies he had hired in the meantime. In consideration for the inconvenience, the innkeeper proposed a banquet to be held in the courtyard of the inn in William's honor.

"I think it's disgraceful," said Emily.

"Oh, I wouldn't say that. The man's trying to be fair."

"No, I think it's disgraceful that you've accepted. It's beneath your dignity to get involved in such pettiness."

There were times when his wife's directness bothered William. He always did his best not to let it.

"A veteran of more than six years, Emily, and still you don't know these Chinese. Face is everything, you must know that. I'd lose a good deal more by refusing than I will by playing along.

"Face. That's what it's all about and I can tell you this much: without face you and I would've been hounded out of this city on our very first day."

"And what if to save this peculiarly intangible *face* of yours you were being asked to accept not a banquet but the thief's hand, his actual, severed, bloodied hand? It's been known to happen."

"But my love," William spoke gently but with all the chilling patience of the pedagogue, "that isn't what I'm being asked. It's a perfectly civil and civilized gesture of atonement. Trivial maybe, and not something we'd want in our own country, but it isn't wrong. They're a very childlike people and if we want to live here comfortably we'll just have to swallow our pride and become like them."

Emily held back her next words. She had been about to remind William of his own words to Martha on the subject of becoming like the people but she knew he would begin to discuss the differences and the appalling ignorance of the mountain villagers. Emily knew that any discussion of Martha's circumstances would be bound to end in the truth coming out, and she did not want that just now. There was still time to pry Martha out of her village.

"You're probably right," she said. "But I still think it's rather unfair of you to go all that way." She smiled crookedly. "A whole day and a night, you know. For face."

"Oh, come on now. You'll not be by yourself. You've got Chiang and Lin-sao and James, not to mention Edward. He keeps you busy enough."

"Yes, and he's not looking too well today. There's another reason for you to stay."

"Ah, you mustn't blackmail me with the children. If he's sick, my love, when I'm gone you have a whole pharmacy at your fingertips. Stop worrying."

He kissed her on the forehead, the way adults kiss small children.

William returned from the banquet as soon as he could. His conscience was a cumbersome machine, too slow for his uncompromising actions but too ponderous to stop once it had begun to work. All too often he condemned his own conduct after the event, so that while to others he seemed to be a man of long consideration and firm action, he was in fact plagued by a pattern of impulse followed by self-recrimination. Now, against the charge of neglect of his wife and children, William's conscience brought down its familiar verdict of guilty. It had been a hard decision for him. The claims of the mission — and he considered the banquet to be a positive step towards the promotion of the mission — always weighed heavily on him.

And then there was Miss Coleridge to consider. William had accepted the invitation to the banquet on an impulse, promising himself to go on and visit Martha and persuade her to come down to Tsehchow. Now his equally hasty reversal meant more recriminations; and the problem of Martha remained.

Not far from the city, the road turned sharply to the east, skirting an ancient well. William pulled up his mule abruptly. The scavenger dogs were there again, scrabbling at the walls of the well and yelping in frustration. William dismounted and reached for some loose rocks. He hurled stone after stone at the animals until they moved off and then he turned and knelt down and prayed. Into the well behind him, the most desperate of the city's poor, lowered, gently lowered in wicker baskets, their unnamed, unwanted, and — God be thanked — unknowing babies. William prayed for mercy for the infants, for the parents; he prayed for the children of China, for the people of the world. And as his prayers ringed outward from that evil-smelling place, his anger calmed.

The mule had wandered away. William climbed down the slope on the other side of the road and found the animal waiting to be caught again. He mounted and rode on, his thoughts gradually returning to his own children. There would have been more, but there had been miscarriages, a stillbirth. He sometimes wondered if there were things he should, or should not, have done.

When he arrived at the compound, he called Chiang to see to the mule. James was there running backwards and forwards across the courtyard, tugging on invisible reins in front of him and making a raucous screech in the back of his throat, like the sound of new wheels.

"Where's your mother, James?"

James reined to a stop and pointed with an imaginary whip before he made off again in the direction of the smaller court to the side.

"Is Madam in the surgery, Chiang?"

"Yes, Doctor. Many people come. T'ai-t'ai say baby not sleep. People make much noise. T'ai-t'ai open surgery and people make quiet." Chiang was quick to see William's anxious glances towards the bedrooms. "Baby sleep," he said reassuringly. "Lin-sao have baby."

"Tell Madam to close up now." William made his way through to the wide inner courtyard. The family rooms here each opened onto the wooden veranda that ran around three sides of the paved court. He saw that the shades were down on Edward's window and stopped to listen. No crying. Only a distant, low crooning. Opening the door gently, he paused while his eyes adjusted to the darkness; then he saw Lin-sao kneeling and the baby Edward not in his cradle but lying still and quiet on the table.

William flung back the door, startling Lin-sao so that she scrambled to her feet, knocking over a bowl of black liquid as she reached to snuff the incense that burned by Edward's head.

"What in God's name are you doing, woman?" William pushed her aside so roughly that she brought up her arms as if to ward off blows and hid her face behind the heavy sleeves of her gown while he looked at the baby.

The eyes were closed over an expression of unmistakable

agony. The face was drawn, drained of color. Although a cold and slimy sweat streaked the small limbs, they were not covered. William saw that the soles of the baby's feet had been painted a deep purple-black; he looked the child over carefully and turned incredulous eyes on the old amah.

"What have you done, Lin-sao?"

"Not Lin-sao. Not Lin-sao," she said, shaking and shaking her head like a small child. "Not Lin-sao. Devil make. Devil make." Her eyes were watery with shame and hurt.

"You — " William shut his mouth tight on the words and held his breath until it burst from him in a snort of anger. He went to the door and shouted at the top of his voice, making the tiny figure in his arms twitch convulsively.

"Chiang!"

There was a clang of dropped buckets and the boy came running across the courtyard.

"Here," William pulled the wrappings awkwardly round the baby and placed him in Chiang's arms. "Put baby in bed. Baby sleep. Nobody come touch," he added, looking at Lin-sao mopping the black fluid from the floor.

Emily had closed the street door when William came into the surgery. She was standing at the dispensing table sorting out the used bottles. Limp feathers of her red hair hung about her face and the dark rings were there again around her eyes. She looked up and her luxurious sense of relief at William's return was gone in a moment.

"What's the matter?" she began.

But already William's voice came, scorching and acid. *What's the matter?* You tell me, Madam, what the matter is. You stand here, my Lady Bountiful, dispensing our good medicine to those heathens while that witch out there practices her black magic on my son."

He turned from her in disgust and began searching the shelves of jars and bottles.

"William — " Emily had no time to ask what he meant before he continued.

"God be praised I came home when I did. It's a miracle the child isn't dead already. I would have — "

"What are you saying?" Emily pulled at William's arm as he reached for a bottle of quinine.

"Cholera, Emily, that's what I'm saying."

He turned and looked down at her face and saw the incomprehension there. And then it left her. "No," she said under her breath, and turned and ran from the room.

Edward was dead before midnight.

Emily sat by his cradle quietly. She could still hear William's rage beating blindly about the room, angry words that verged on blasphemy, and she knew now that as he sat in his room his Bible would be unopened under his clenched fist and he would have no words to pray. She tried to pray for him and the words came. The shock of Edward's death had been for Emily an explosion that had shattered her faith, her duty, and left the pieces plastered to her body. There was nothing inside any more to complicate the words she had to say.

"O Lord, have pity on Thy weak and frail servants in their sorrow." She asked for grace to understand, divine light to see. "If we seem to falter and to faint in our acceptance of the glorious will of God, forgive us, Lord, and extend Thy mercies to us. Hear us when we say Thy will be done."

One of the candles beside the cradle guttered and went out. Emily found another and lit it. Her hands remembered for her the infinite grace of Lin-sao's thick hands as she lit her wands of incense. Emily had seen that gesture. She was ashamed that she had not been able to tell everything to William but he had been all anger and his voice had been like a great shout murdering her own.

She had seen Lin-sao lighting her forbidden incense. From the doorway she had seen her draw a paper from her sleeve and unfold it and place it, with its painted image of an idol, between the wands. She had seen all that and then she had crept away from Edward's room, knowing that the baby slept and that Lin-sao loved him enough to pray for him.

Emily had *not* seen the amah unwrap the baby and paint the soles of his feet with the dragon's blood, to draw the sickness down through his body. But what if she had? As a mother she would have protested, but as a Christian? What right had she to be angry? Lin-sao had acted out of compassion, going to the god she knew best.

Edward was dead. Nothing could change that. It had nothing to do with Lin-sao. With China perhaps, with dirt and flies and lice, but not with Lin-sao. Emily remembered how the old woman's jaw had been shaking as she tried to explain her actions to William. And yet her motives were the same as William's: to bend the will of God. We're all the same, thought Emily. We see the hand of God begin to move and we fight and we struggle and we plead and we try to turn it from us. And Lin-sao trying not for herself even, but for Edward. Out of love. She, a heathen, knows Christ's message: *All men between the four seas are brothers.* Does she need to hear it again in a foreign tongue?

Emily would not answer her own question. She knelt down and prayed beside the cradle until she heard the watchman call the last hour before dawn.

The weeks that followed drained away darkly into winter. The problem of Martha was slowly buried under the piling snow. William and Emily, in their self-imposed quarantine, paced and prayed and watched James nervously for signs of sickness. But James, who let all kinds of unsavory material past his lips, raced through the house still.

The servants, too, were treated to incarceration and they, too, prayed — for quick release from the mandatory diet of thick canned milk and potted ham. Chiang eyed the two big crates with disgust, counting the number of cans yet to be ingested before the quarantine was over and he could get back to the market again.

At last the waiting drew to a close and the family knew they were out of danger. But the long, aching days of sadness and self-recrimination had left their mark. William and Emily had slept together only once in their sadness and only in a clumsy, unhappy attempt at consolation. When the quarantine ended, they kept their mutual isolation like a covenant. By day they worked in silence and at night they lay apart in their bed, both afraid to find in each other the signs of faltering

69

confidence they found in themselves.

William's raging against Edward's death had been real enough, was at least an affirmation that his God existed, nearer, more powerful than ever before. But Emily, accustomed to speaking only to other people's gods in other people's polite phrases, was alarmed by the raw outburst; she tried to temper it with convention and a proper reverence. It was then, when William heard her praying, using words he had sprinkled often and carelessly on others in their sorrow, that his hold on his own faith slipped just a little. He wanted to hear the sounds of a mother's grief coming from Emily's lips and instead he heard the familiar trite phrases worn thin and featureless by constant use, borrowed currency given back by all those who did not really know their God and needed words to say for saying's sake.

And the words, after all, were nothing more than words? The question chilled him. He tried to warm himself with work, re-opening the surgery and the church, but his busyness turned to restlessness and nothing would shift it. He would leave letters unfinished, close the surgery early, postpone visits. Towards the people he was increasingly intolerant and his preaching bristled with bad-tempered hectoring. The congregation dwindled and those that remained, for reasons of their own, closed their ears to this discourteous barbarian maiming their language with his foreign tongue.

Emily watched all this and was shocked, but like a visitor to a sickbed she maintained a stubborn cheerfulness. Neither of them spoke about it. The shadow of the unspoken question remained. William had no voice for doubt — it would have choked him.

As his restlessness turned to dissatisfaction, William cast about for excuses. How could he admit after six years that he was not fitted for China? He found an explanation in his health; he told himself the poor living conditions had taken their toll, his spirit was drained, a little fortification was all he needed. A tonic — that was it. In his depressed state, the idea appealed to William, and he began to take occasional draughts of morphine. Only small amounts, he argued, would be necessary, but their effect would be of enormous value, make a world of difference in his work.

William had reached his decision in the surgery one day as they were finishing. He was turning to tell Emily that he was going to make up a tonic for himself, when he changed his mind, telling her instead that he had a special order to make up for the next day. It seemed better not to give her too much to think about right now, especially if, as he had begun to suspect, she were carrying another child — it seemed likely even though there was only that one sad time since Edward's death.

Weeks later, as he was making up a small supply of his restorative, congratulating himself on its success, William was again on the point of speaking to Emily, wondering if she herself might not do well to take a dose. But then again his health was much improved and she made no complaint about her own — she was almost certainly carrying another child. No point bothering her with troubles that were all over with.

As the winter months passed, Emily saw a change in William: where once he was restless, he became quiet and complacent. She did not understand these moods but she accepted them. He still left work unfinished, walking out abstractedly from his office, a sermon lying half-written on the table, but he seemed to be at peace. On certain evenings he would sit for hours, silently musing, his chair pulled up to the lamp, his book on his lap, unopened.

At nights William and Emily lay awake together, not touching. William would stare for long hours into the darkness on those nights, his eyes wide open, only his body sleeping, not moving when Emily turned over, not starting when a slide of snow made its sudden hissing rush from the roof into the silence. His mind rocked softly, lulled by waves of morphine.

Emily had no way of knowing William's secret; she knew only that he no longer needed her, so that she was left alone now with her aching body, remembering. At first she lay sleepless beside him. Sometimes she would reach for William's hand and pull it to her rounded belly; his eyes would close

71

but his hand would lie heavily until she pushed it away and turned and tried to sleep.

After many nights Emily learned not to wait, not to expect. She lay on her side then with her knees drawn up and her hand pressed between her thighs and she imagined, more than she remembered. She imagined herself with William until she could no longer bear the ache and then she would get up and go to be alone and caress the pain until it went away. And soon even the memory of William was not necessary and the pain itself was what she longed for so that all she needed was the thought, the image of her own hand, caressing.

March 1900, Jun-ch'eng

It was warm inside Martha's room in the mud-walled house. She had a pile of books to repair and she was kneeling on a rush mat on the floor, cutting strips of cotton. When she had enough, she took a dish of glue and a small wooden spatula and spread the glue thinly on the cloth. Picking up a strip she began to press it carefully to the spine of a tattered book. She was concentrating on turning in the ends when she realized that the noise and commotion she had been hearing indistinctly from the village had now arrived at her own walls. She looked up as her door opened to a flood of spring sunshine that darkened almost at once.

William was there, looking in.

Throwing down the book, Martha jumped up and ran to him and was clinging to him, tight against his chest, before he had moved. Instinctively, William closed his arms round her and stood bewildered while her happiness rocked them both. Brushing tears from her eyes and laughing, Martha pulled away to close the door on the courtyard, where her cook, Tang, was still arguing with the crowd outside who wanted another look at the tall, gaunt foreigner.

"Well! I hardly know what to say . . . I'm not used to people bursting in all unannounced like this!" William missed the irony but smiled anyway. "See what a disturbance you are, when I'm busy!"

He watched, still smiling, as she pulled a swatch of sticky cotton from the sole of her slipper.

"There. I'll have to get this finished before the children come for class. Sit down, sit down," she said pointing at the hearth. "Tell me how you all find yourselves. How is Emily?"

"She's well." As if this were a weight of information, William nodded heavily. "Yes, very well."

"I'm glad, but that won't do at all. How *is* she? Is she liking the city as much as Lin-an? And the children? Oh, little Edward. Has he come out of his rush basket yet, the little dormouse? He looked as if he'd sleep in that nest all his life."

Tang came in to make tea. He set up a small iron brazier on the hearth next to William and filled it with some of the glowing coals from the fire-box. When he had hung the kettle over it he sat down on the floor to wait. William felt himself excused from answering Martha. Later, when her excitement was calmed by the smoky fragrance of the tea, he told her about Edward but nothing more. Holding to his purpose, he tried to persuade her to join them in Tsehchow.

"Oh no, you mustn't be so pressing on that subject, Doctor. I do very well here. I do. I love it." She was quieter now and it was obvious that she meant what she said. "It's almost perfect."

"Almost?"

"There! You're looking for trouble. I have everything I need. I promise you there's nothing I want."

"I can't believe that," said William, looking round the bare room. "Not up here."

"No, it's true. In fact, I'm worried about someone else altogether but to be perfectly honest it does affect me indirectly because I can't sleep at night for thinking about it. Now, what on earth are you thinking with that terrible expression? You're alarmed — but don't be. It's all over." William sat rigidly, afraid that she was going to tell him everything she had told Emily. His fixed stare left her no choice but to go on. "Well,

73

I'll tell you. Mr. Tang — you know, my very dear cook — he was attacked. No, I said don't be alarmed. It's a great muddle. He told me, to lessen my anxiety I think, that they were trying to rob him. But I don't think so. Poor man, I hardly give him enough to live on as it is. No, I think it was pure malice. We've never been liked here by a certain group of people."

William knew that if he really were ignorant about the initial assault on Martha he should now be asking *why, what people?* But he left the matter alone: making her tell it would be a second violation.

"But then that's all the more reason for you to come away," he said.

"Oh, no. One's not being liked is no reason to run away."

"But if you're attacked . . ."

"But I wasn't. Oh, I know it was meant for me. It's what they'd *like* to do to me but they would never dare. Not now. I'm the Crazy Sister, you see. They're far too scared of my madness to be of any danger to me." Martha spoke without a trace of sarcasm.

"That's rubbish."

"No, it's true. And that's exactly why I can't sleep at nights. I know I'm a cause of trouble and it's Mr. Tang who pays for my presence here, but I can't leave, not without wasting all the work I've done. And however much I try, I can't persuade Mr. Tang to leave me."

William's patience was wearing thin. He took a deep breath. "Well, if that's all you're worrying about you might just as well come away and leave the man in peace; it's his village, after all."

But he knew as well as Martha that Tang would find no other work after living with the foreign she-devil. And Martha, as he expected, would have none of it. She changed the subject to a discussion of Tang's culinary marvels and the mysteries of his economy and, by veering sharply into an account of the harshness of the winter, she managed to keep talking until the children arrived.

There were not many. They sat with Martha beside the

hearth, wriggling and fidgeting and craning their necks to look at William again as she told them stories. When the stories were over, Tang brought in a basket of millet cakes. The children snatched at them and ran laughing and pushing out of the house.

When William left, nothing had changed.

His decision to see Martha had been sudden, taken one March morning when the cold had left off gnawing hands and feet and the people had removed their topmost layer of quilting and smiled in the sun. Sensing the change, the newness in the air, William had felt as if the doors of his mind had been flung open to the light. He searched in the brightness for the purpose he had last put down and found it.

Emily had not minded his going. She had been glad to see their obligation to Martha Coleridge finally honored. There had been rumors through the winter of the Crazy Sister's night-walking. Besides, William had promised that he wouldn't stay away long.

Now, returning, he rode all night with the frost glittering in the moonlight and the ground ringing hard under his pony's hooves. The air was so raw that his lips were numb, but he did not stop. At dawn he reached the mountain temple that was inhabited by a solitary monk. The holy man led a remarkably social existence for a hermit, offering a resting place for travellers using the pass, and learning incidentally things about most people in the town. William stopped there to water his pony and take a drink himself and then he rode on to Tsehchow without stopping again.

His thoughts were occupied with Martha. What he had seen on this visit in the spring sunlight could not begin to obliterate what he thought he had heard on that September night. His visions disgusted him but he could not get rid of them, the bodies jerking and the hands mauling. And it was impossible not to weigh the work she did against the risks she took. She was living, still, in the threat of the most extreme harm. And for what? A row of round greedy faces; dimpled hands that snatched at a basket of millet cakes. But isn't that what they were doing out here, handing out millet cakes, of

75

one kind or another?

William preferred to let these bubbles of thought rest undisturbed where they had risen and concentrated again on Martha's troubles. If she wouldn't leave, and it was obvious no one could make her, then at least she ought to look after herself. She had to sleep, that went without saying, or her health would break down completely. William decided at once what he should do.

On his return to the mission, he greeted Emily briefly and went straight to the surgery. He unlocked the dispensary cupboard, mixed and bottled a quantity of his morphine draught sufficient in nightly doses for two weeks, corked and labelled the two bottles writing Martha's name and then, after some consideration, the words *Somnific Restorative*, and set them aside on a shelf. When he had taken his own draught, he closed up the surgery again.

In the bedroom Chiang had made ready some hot water and laid out clean clothes. William washed the dirt of the journey from himself, changed, and joined his wife and son in the small room where they took their meals.

Emily learned without surprise that there had been more violence but that Martha would not come down. "She's a different breed, William. Tsehchow to Martha would be the lap of luxury. Remember Lin-an? She'd be the same here. Like a wild horse in a drawing room."

"Maybe. But I never did shirk responsibility, you know that."

Emily wondered whether William knew the whole of Martha's story now. If she had told him this other thing, about the attack on Tang, it was quite probable.

"So what do you suggest?" she said.

"I can look after her health, for one thing," said William.

"Well you won't have much to do. Martha has a constitution of iron. I've never known such a woman."

"Not nearly as strong as you think, my dear. I'm making up a tonic for her with something to cure her insomnia. In fact, I should probably take it to her tomorrow."

Emily had her fork halfway to her lips. She slowly replaced

it on her plate and looked up at William across the table. "Tomorrow."

"Yes, my dear." William wiped his mouth and pushed his plate aside with deliberate finality. He sat back with an expression quite unmoved. Objective.

"Come with me, James." Emily brushed the crumbs of food from James's clothes. "We must find Lin-sao," she said. "Please excuse us, William." She handed James over to his amah without listening to his chatter and walked away as he was still talking to her.

In the kitchen Emily took out the account books and prepared for an evening's work. The pages lay open but her mind would not engage them. She stared at the columns of figures drawn up by Chiang and the pencil in her hand did not move. Finally, without knowing why, she got up and went to the surgery. There seemed to be something underhanded about unlocking the door and going to the cupboard for no reason; she felt extraordinarily guilty.

There. The two bottles stood side by side on the shelf. Emily took them down, a clean freshly written label on each: *Miss Coleridge*. William really did mean to go tomorrow. The draught was already made up. The fact that her husband had mixed it before he had been in the house for as much as ten minutes — and after riding all night — was not lost on Emily. It might have been written there in careful copperplate on the offending labels.

As she put back the bottles, Emily pursed her lips. There was a grittiness to her resentment, something more like defiance. She closed up again, slamming the doors as if she meant to bang them in the face of her own unnecessary guilt at being there. She went back to the kitchen and sat staring crossly at the books.

William had no business visiting Martha. There were a hundred other ways of helping her; dozens of ways to get medicines to her. What did William want, going up there again? Like an invalid rearranging pillows around herself, Emily began to adjust her opinions and her attitudes to ease her pain. It was improper, Martha living alone there and it was unjust of William to devote so much of his time to her welfare. Wasn't she, Emily, in as much danger when William was away? City or village, did it make any difference to a woman unprotected? Her own confinement was little more than four months away now. Martha should come down if she was unwell. She should put aside her eccentric predilections and start thinking of others for a change and all the worry she was causing. She should start behaving like a normal person.

Emily closed the book with a bang and left. Outside James's room she consciously slowed her step and took a deep breath to calm herself. When she went in to say goodnight to him she looked as calm as always. In her own room the flood of words against William and Martha gathered into a single pounding wave: *Go then. Go then. Go then.*

That evening William remained comfortably oblivious of Emily's reaction, largely because of her silence but partly too because she had encouraged his first visit. He had no way of inferring her objections unless she chose to tell him, and this she did not even consider; his gesture with the plate was, as she well knew, his signal that the matter was decided. William was skilled at transmitting such signals but particularly poor at receiving them — unless they were the ones he hoped to hear. When Emily had risen stiffly from the table and left him without further discussion, utter lack of interest was the only message he received. It was all very convenient.

Emily flung a thick shawl round her shoulders and went with William to the main gate of the compound. There she politely wished him a good journey and turned to tack up a notice announcing the mission's temporary closure. Today being the Festival of One Thousand Harmonies, William had agreed that it would be a good idea not to open. It was not that either of them were afraid of any particular trouble, but William had his reservations: "When these people get together, you never can tell; there's no banking on manners here, you know." And so as soon as it was light, Emily had gone to the desk in the office, taken brush and ink and copied from her

78

battered copy of Wade the characters of her notice.

It hardly mattered that her efforts were more artistic than accurate; the brief respite from duty that the notice represented kept her from losing patience. Her own lack of guilt at stealing time for herself in this way surprised her. But then if William could spare the time . . .

In fact, there was some spiteful satisfaction in balancing her own self-indulgence against his. She might as well acknowledge the luxury it was to be able to indulge the bovine complacency of her confinement without William's melancholic moonings. And in what exactly was William about to indulge? She hoped it was nothing more than idle escape from a routine turned tedious, nothing more than a social exchange with a face other than her own. Nothing more.

Emily went inside to the sheltered courtyard and found James playing in the sunshine while Lin-sao washed the breakfast bowls. He had a small dish of water. She knelt down on the stones beside him but he continued his game, carefully dropping pebbles into the dish and watching with absorption as the water overflowed. Emily sighed softly. James would grow to be a strange little creature, isolated, living behind walls, locked gates. She felt the shape of the baby, high under her ribs — tried to picture it but saw only Edward's tiny face.

"Lin-sao," she called, "I think we should watch the procession today." Emily always spoke in Mandarin to her servants but they invariably answered in pidgin, enjoying the novelty of manipulating this new language. Lin-sao answered that master had said to stay home.

"The master isn't here," said Emily and then, coming to the door and mimicking, "Master gone walkee-walkee." Lin-sao laughed with a sound like crackling paper and scooped up the bowls onto the shelf in one alarming motion.

Between them the women persuaded Chiang to keep his disapproval to himself and stay behind to take care of the compound. Lin-sao helped Emily to dress as inconspicuously as possible. They wrapped themselves in layer upon layer and Emily covered her red hair with a scarf wound round and round like a peasant woman's. James as always wore a little padded jacket and trousers like the other children; today Lin-sao made him wear the round cap that hid his thick, wavy hair.

The festival crowds that filled the wide main street had time for nothing but the brass bells that they hung from sticks and strung from poles between them; they tied and retied them, changed them, exchanged them and bickered endlessly, happily, over the finer points of their chimes. Lin-sao bought a bell for James and then she led them in through the garden of a temple and up some stairs cut in the wall to a little tower. Here the three of them could sit and watch, out of the jostling crowd, while the blur of color and sound began to open like a paper flower and find its shape.

Behind the roar of excitement came an inchoate ringing beat. It detached itself, it grew louder, and finally like the insistent, beating wings of a giant bird it caught up all other sounds in its own momentum; the bronze chimes, the bamboo rattles, gongs, drums, all fell in with the swelling beat beneath the constant ringing of the air. Only the firecrackers defied it.

James jumped excitedly, his feet answering the beat, so that Lin-sao had to hang on to the back of his jacket to keep him from precipitating himself down into the crowd. As they watched, the mass of people began to move apart, clearing a path in the centre of the street for the wild tangle of color that, twisting and tumbling, loomed towards them. The giant gongs heralding the approach of the dragon were near enough to see. Men with silk streamers snaking after them swayed under the great weight.

"The monster! The monster!" shrieked James.

Ponderous, elaborate, the dragon tossed its shaggy head and lashed its long body as it progressed. Every inch of its red and purple surface was hung with silver bells, their chimes drowned by the tremendous noise. Firecrackers split the air in its wake so that James now shrieked in earnest and buried his face against Lin-sao's shoulders. Emily watched as the last of the dancers was engulfed by the crowd spilling again throughout the street. It was as if the dragon had driven all

80

the excitement before it, the firecrackers burning off the remnants.

Food vendors settled in whatever spaces they could find, lighted their fires and started cooking. Could one really call them wicked, or lost, or damned? Emily wondered. Were they sinning now? William would say the whole affair was rooted in idolatry. Did she believe that? They were poor. They needed western science and medicine. Did they need guilt too, the knowledge of sin? All her teaching answered for her: yes, they must acknowledge the guilt and be saved.

"Come along, James. No more monster. No more fire."

James took his hands from his ears and said with false bravado, "I hope it comes back again."

Emily smiled and took his hand. "Let's walk," she said. They climbed down from the wall and made their way slowly through the crowded streets. Soon they lost themselves in the noise and the laughter all around them, the sea of faces swirling above James's head. Emily felt the loneliness of the stranger. She didn't belong and had no wish to. But, she asked herself, if it were not for saving souls, then for what, exactly, did she stay? Knowing where it led, Emily put aside the question, and concentrated on James's amusement.

They returned home as the sky was darkening and the people were drifting from the empty food stalls. Near the compound, on a patch of wasteland where a ruined building stood, they came upon a group of children playing. James stopped at the sight of the lighted tapers they held and watched, remembering another celebration, as they tried to ignite a bundle of straws. The straws were tied into a shape they called their dragon.

Emily put her hand on Lin-sao's arm to forestall her scolding and watched as James bent down beside the boy who conducted the operation. They were absorbed in their self-appointed task. As the legs of the dragon-doll began to burn, the children laughed uproariously, not watching even to the end but beginning to push and pull at each other in the first moves of a giant melee.

Suddenly James was recognized for the first time. Darting

forward, the smallest boy snatched at his cap. James's thatch of wavy hair was exposed and the children hooted with delight. Emily drew James away and the noise of the jeering dropped to a low murmur. As they walked away James looked back constantly. The tight knot of panic he had felt loosened into strands of bewilderment. The insults he had caught were full of scorn and revulsion. *"Huai tan! Huai tan! Ni shi shenmo tungshi?"* He could not understand why they were meant for him.

Emily was in a rage. She hated everything around her now. Unreasonably, she hated in particular Lin-sao shuffling clumsily beside her; and when Chiang opened the gates and began his polite enquiries about the outing she hated him, too. Speaking in a tight, controlled voice she dismissed the two servants, telling them the rest of the holiday was theirs to enjoy at will.

Alone now, Emily fed the boy herself and put him to bed as soon as it was dark. She could not bear to have him near her, preferring to pamper her own bitterness. She went into the drawing room but its rugs and screens and lacquered furniture that had delighted her in Lin-an only disgusted her. All the rooms were the same. She wrapped herself in a hide blanket and went out to the long veranda that connected all the rooms around the inner courtyard.

The night was bright with a big moon ringed by a whitish haze, like the breath of winter lingering. Emily sat on the veranda step and leaned against the gnarled stem of an old wisteria that grew around the pillar. Listening to the muted noises from the city, she wanted to take up her execration of all things Chinese — but she could not. The country, the people, the mission were all tainted for her but, removed from them, Emily was no longer angry, only sad. She put her hatred away, tucked it tidily in reserve for William — and perhaps Martha.

It was an irony of which neither ever became aware, that the hatred Emily conceived that night did William the greatest service of his life. Throughout the month, Emily harbored that resentment darkly, wordlessly, like a mother with a

82

malformed child. At the end of March, William made a third visit to Martha taking, discreetly, a further two weeks' supply of his tonic for her. It was then, on her husband's return, that Emily's creature demanded deliverance.

"I trust you had a fruitful journey," she said late that night when she found William in the stable unsaddling the pony.

"One that had to be made, at any rate," said William, picking up a bunch of straw and beginning to rub the pony's neck.

"Oh, really? Something especially urgent that takes you to Jung-ch'eng so often?" William swung around. "More urgent, I mean, than mission business? A mad woman in the mountains?"

"Martha's a co-worker. In God's field, if you remember. Kindly treat her with some respect."

"Respect? Oh, I've every respect for *Martha* — as you've taken to calling her. It's you I wonder about, William. What is it exactly that keeps you trotting up there after her? Don't tell me you're concerned for her safety. She survived the winter, didn't she, without your help."

"You're making yourself ridiculous. You begin to sound like a jealous woman."

"Jealous! I'm *anxious!* I'm an anxious wife and mother who sees her husband, her child's father, riding out into the mountains when he should be here at home. Where his duty lies."

"My first duty is to the mission and its workers."

"And what am I? I suppose it's all right for you to go away and leave me to cope with every crisis single-handed?"

William looked sharply at Emily, not sure whether this was her trump card or another of her exaggerations.

"Oh, yes. We had a crisis here while you were out visiting. Some of the men from the town arrested that new convert. Said he hadn't paid his dues. But there's a crisis of some kind or another nearly every day. Or haven't you noticed? And the rumors are getting worse and worse."

"But Emily, that's surely why I have to go up to Miss Coleridge."

"No. If you were really concerned you'd order her to come down. Your visits make no difference at all. I know why you go."

"That's enough. This is some figment of your childish imagination and you insult me with it. Deeply."

"Yes, and I'll go on insulting you, William, until you act in a way that deserves more respect." There was no door for Emily to slam, although she would have dearly liked one; she contented herself with storming across the courtyard and opening the door on the other side with a bang that woke James.

William left the pony and sat down on a bale of straw. In the silence he came upon his real motives for going to Martha. Reluctantly he conceded, somewhere in the tangle of his self-justification, that he had begun to need companionship in his addiction and there, startlingly, was the admission that he would never otherwise have been able to make — that he was, indeed, addicted to morphine.

From the moment of that admission William's recovery was assured.

April 1900, Tsehchow

The clerk led William through a succession of silent ante-chambers, each one bare except for perhaps a screen or a mahogany table or a single outsized vase. Somewhere outside, to their right, William could hear a man's voice shouting orders, and, once, the sound of steel clashing. The clerk stopped at a door that opened to the central courtyard; he made a point of waiting, staring straight ahead down the passage, until William had taken in the scene outside.

About thirty men were assembled there. In a strange parody of military drill, they stepped and wheeled, lunged and fenced, moving to the commands with slow grace, sometimes stopping abruptly, sometimes letting one gesture flow into another but always with precision, with deliberation. Martial dancers in an eerie ballet. Red ribbons fluttered from their wrists in the dry wind. They wore the yellow sashes of the I Ho Ch'uan, the Fists of Righteous Harmony, and their queues were lashed around their heads, ready for action.

As William watched, the Boxers drew their swords and the measure of the movement changed. They swung the heavy weapons two-handed at their opponents' necks, swinging, ducking as the other returned the blow, swinging, ducking, gaining momentum at each stroke, faster and faster until they obliterated themselves in a whirl of color. William saw now, for the first time, the tableau behind the performance; across the court, in the shade of a terrace, sat the district magistrate, immobile and splendid in his full ceremonial brocade, beside him two Boxers standing in place of the guard of honor.

The clerk continued down the passage and William followed — not, as he had expected, to join the magistrate and have the whole insulting display of belligerence rammed down his throat, but to wait in the reception hall where, he supposed, he had to reflect on it all in solitude. The meaning of the exhibition was obvious. All year, rumors had been increasing about bands of men, secret sects and guilds that pledged themselves to the overthrow of the Manchu and the destruction of the foreigner. Of these groups, the Boxers, revolutionary in purpose and xenophobic in practice, had caused the greatest stir, not in the imperial palaces, but in western circles. However scornful the *North China Herald* liked to be about the tactics of the group, there was no denying its existence, or its intent; and there were Boxers right here in Tsehchow.

What prompted William to deeper thought, however, was their presence in this central courtyard in the very heart of the yamen and under the auspices of a servant of that same dynasty they claimed they were trying to overthrow. That the entire display had been staged for his benefit, he was quite sure. It was an oblique indication that his influence in official quarters was waning fast and that his mission here in Tsehchow was a matter of the utmost indifference to the magistrate, Wu.

William despised the devious nature of the insult. Wu, it seemed, wanted him out but he didn't have the courage to admit it. A cowardly contrivance: it allowed Wu to affront his honor by disclosing anti-foreign demonstrations in the official residence, the seat of hospitality; at the same time, it protected the man from the charge of personal animosity that would have certainly attached to an invitation to attend. William found himself without grounds for protest; a 'chance' discovery of a private exercise was not enough.

Although he had no doubts about what he was expected to infer, William was not certain of the magistrate's true political sympathies. He couldn't understand how Wu, a creature of the imperial machine, could seriously entertain the objectives of the Boxers, unless he was himself a rebel. The Boxers were the poorest of men and William knew that the price of the magistrate's patronage would be too high; they couldn't possibly have bought his favor. What then if *he* had bought *them*? The significance of such a possibility was not lost on William. The rebels must have been offering something the magistrate badly wanted. Not, certainly, the destruction of the very state that supported him. Then — William articulated the conclusion he had drawn intuitively at the sight of the two factions together — then the service they were to provide, and which the magistrate — he did not doubt — had bought, was the expulsion, the destruction of the foreign devil.

Finding the idea more than plausible, William eagerly cast about for support for it; however chilling, such a conclusion would nevertheless allow him the gratification of branding the magistrate once and for all a treacherous enemy. When they had first arrived in the city, Wu had shown some sympathy for the missionaries and had extended his personal protection, despite considerable pressure from the prefect to get them out of the district before they could settle. His attitude until now had been impeccable.

William began to suspect the cause of this elaborate insult.

The mission had recently acquired a new piece of property. William had fully expected Wu to use his privilege to pre-empt the deal and sell to him at a higher price. As it happened, all that Wu had gained in the course of William's transaction with the vendor was extra work for himself in settling the disputes that inevitably followed. Wu had made plain his displeasure at the whole venture, plain, at least, as the demands of protocol would allow. At the time, William had crowed over his swift success in the deal; now, recalling the Boxer posters he had noticed fluttering from the doorway of the vendor's own shop, he wished that he had rested content with their original premises.

By the time William reached this stage in his mental fingering of the evidence, the conclusion he drew needed no coaxing: the I Ho Ch'uan were in the pay of the magistrate; the same pieces of silver that deflected the danger to Wu had transferred it to himself. The initial purpose of his visit to the yamen — to investigate the rumored appointment of a hostile governor in the provincial capital to the north — began to assume a dangerous irony.

"Please sit, please sit, please sit." Wu was already speaking as he entered the room, anxious to establish his ascendancy before William had time to cloud the issue.

"Your Excellency." William bowed, waiting to see if the magistrate's next words would spare him the chore of the customary preamble.

They did not. With half his mind trying to calculate the most appropriate manner shortly to adopt, William politely, reluctantly, engaged in the compulsory verbal tennis; he answered questions about his digestion, his recent illness, his father's health, his son's health, all the time maintaining the proper balance of literalness and outright falsehood — and the correct degree of self-deprecation.

"Yes, Excellency, my humble father is wholly blessed in mind and body with unnaturally good health, which his contemptuous son could never hope to enjoy.

"No, Excellency, my mean and despicable son is now undeservedly well and a source of humble joy to his lowly father . . ." Surely that's enough, William thought.

"You must want something," said Wu.

Through a meticulous process of question and answer, the

two men had constructed a delicate house of words as a preamble to the subject at hand; now Wu, tired of the exercise, had brushed the thing aside, catching William by surprise.

"Your humble servant asks nothing," said William, trying to quell an image of red-ribboned swords. "He comes only to honor your Excellency and to rejoice at your fortune in the good news that emanates from the great capital, T'ai-yüan fu."

Wu was amazed that this foreigner had the hardihood even to allude to imperial affairs, but he showed no surprise. "'The good news'?"

"Is it not ordained that the great Yü Hsien will watch and rule over us from the noble city of T'ai-yüan?"

Wu could hardly believe what he was hearing. Yü Hsien meant nothing but trouble; he was a sore on the inflamed body of internal politics. Didn't this Westerner have any diplomacy? "It is ordained," he said.

"Then I rejoice in the coming prosperity and happiness of the people of Shansi."

William was rapidly confirming Wu's impression of him as a naive blunderer. It was common knowledge that Yü Hsien had been relegated to Shansi after the fiasco in Shantung, where he had behaved more like a thug than a governor and left the province with a murdered Westerner on its hands. If Doctor Bancroft were really offering this last remark as a clumsy form of flattery, then he was sadly ignorant of the real state of affairs. Delivered by anyone who truly understood the wider implications of Yü's appointment, the remark would verge on sarcasm and could only be received as an insult.

Wu was reasonably sure, however, that William had only his own affairs at heart in seeking information about the new governor. He merely nodded his acknowledgment.

William pressed on. "Doubtless the new viceroy," he said, passing out promotions in his effort to please, "will confer many new privileges and responsibilities on his most estimable proconsul. I beg Your Excellency, therefore, not to overlook the matter of our appointed meetings which are of such benefit to the district and to its mission." Again this artful confusion of an alien religion, and its invidious imposition, with matters of imperial government; Wu did not answer. William waited a moment and continued, "And I beg to offer Your Excellency the attentions of your humble servant in whatever capacity Your Excellency deems fit."

William had no idea how close he stepped to insult. It was a fact that Wu, while resenting the mission's presence in the town for the inconvenience and administrative nuisance it caused, rather admired some of the work the couple performed there in their dispensary; but when one of these uncultured strangers presumed to suggest that he could be of some personal assistance, that he had something to offer, then Wu's dignity was indeed affronted.

"I should not presume to impose upon you in any way whatsoever," he answered stiffly and then, "When are you moving that chapel of yours?"

The shift of tone was unnerving — it was meant to be.

"I do not understand, Excellency."

"That street chapel you've set up. It's got to go. I told you at the last meeting that you'll have to use the building for some other purpose or get out of it. Find somewhere else."

"Of course. I understand," said William, now thoroughly ill at ease and unable to manage this routine issue in his usual way. "Your Excellency need not be concerned. It is already in our minds to move the establishment. Our mission does not seek to offend but to serve. I shall resolve the matter as soon as I can."

"I'm glad you're so cooperative, Doctor Bancroft. I have, of course, no wish to inconvenience you. Now tell me when you will move."

"I have no date fixed as yet . . . these things, I am sure you understand, take time . . ." He took an inspired chance: "I shall need approval from Tientsin."

As William had hoped, the magistrate construed the mention of Tientsin to refer not to the regional headquarters of the mission but to the British consulate there. Exercising considerable restraint, Wu led the conversation deftly away from the subject and into the platitudes that signalled the end of the interview.

William left the yamen as coolly and unhurriedly as he could manage. His first thought was for Emily and the boy — his second for Martha.

Emily's condition made a sudden flight, should it come to that, impractical. William wanted to remove her and the boy to a safer place but he was reluctant to let them go alone; nor was he prepared to spare the servants from their mission work: it wouldn't do if the mission broke down under the first sign of pressure. Then, too, if he used the servants as escorts there was the question of reliability. You might make these Chinamen Christians but that didn't mean you made them honest. For the same reason he rejected the idea of hiring men from the town as escorts; a more politically astute man would have realized that Wu would underwrite any contract with his personal guarantee, just to rid his district of the nuisance of the mission.

The simplest solution to the problem was the most obvious. William himself could escort his family to safety, if it weren't for his pride. And the mission was all his pride. Whatever it had been, or was now, it remained something he couldn't readily abandon; if he couldn't believe that the God he served would protect it, then he could believe in nothing. Face, as William was fond of saying of the Chinese, was indeed everything. His withdrawal now would lay bare the foundation of his whole life. There was no question of his leaving.

In what he considered a satisfactory compromise, William planned to send a courier to telegraph Tientsin. He would find out which other missionaries might be leaving Shansi and then a suitable party could be assembled. Until he found an escort the family would remain together.

Martha must come down, that much was clear. Since his recovery he had wanted to go to her, but a certain cowardice — knowing what he would find there — had held him back. Now he had all the reason he needed for going, without ever having to raise the more sensitive arguments.

It could all be done without upsetting Emily. And heaven forbid he should upset Emily again. She had no idea about

90

Martha's possible state of dependence on his restorative. There wasn't any reason to tell her now. He thanked God Emily had never to know about what he called his own *misfortune* with the drug. All in all, he'd had a God-given deliverance from the whole experience; it could have been worse, he liked to tell himself — especially with a weaker man.

In fact, the course William had to take had been set out for him that night in the stable when he first saw his addiction for what it was. He had tried afterwards to sidestep the terror, asked himself whether rejecting the tonic wasn't just unhealthy self-mortification, whether he might not after all reasonably continue, since the hand of God would surely protect him. But despite these waverings, William did not turn back. On the day that followed his resolution, he succumbed to a violent fever and a nausea that shook his whole frame like a sea-sickness.

Emily waited on him night and day as she would a cholera victim, seeing the dark stains that spread from his neck and shoulders and soaked into the sheets, watching with alarm as his nose and mouth leaked the poisons that seemed to fill him. She listened, frightened, to his ravings about the medicines in the dispensary, and imagined his senses had left him when he screamed to be alone, until in a panic she sent to the yamen for help. The magistrate's physician concurred: William should be left alone.

Afterwards, thankful to find himself whole again so soon, William was in no danger of a second fall from grace: he was protected by the deadliest of sins. There was no self-recrimination; it was a wholly understandable accident of circumstance, a misfortune he had incurred — through no fault of his own.

Only one stubborn discomfort lodged in his conscience: Martha. He couldn't pretend even to himself that she wouldn't have known at least some of the agonies of deprivation that he had just suffered. And yet he had done nothing, had told himself there was nothing he could do, that her suffering without the morphine would be over in the space of a week, that his presence would only increase her torment. It came

91

now as a relief to be able to drop these arguments and take up the reverse position. This new and urgent reason for going to her might be unwelcome but at least it was reassuringly objective. He would bring her down to safety.

As he turned the corner into the long, walled street of the compound, William was stirred by the gallantry of the idea.

Emily sat at her desk arranging and rearranging the piles of papers, the weekly reports, the orders for medical supplies. She had kept one piece of paper folded in her hand for a long time — Dora's letter from Auldbury. Her sister's voice carried to her echoes of comfort and security. It asked why, when they had missed their furlough last year, they were not planning to return home in the summer. Emily read the letter again and then put it in her pocket. William, she knew, had already dismissed the idea of a trip home. She stared blankly at the papers, the book orders, the dockets of the food parcels; waiting for William she could not attend to any of it.

Had the infamous Yü, she was anxious to know, really been appointed governor? The provincial capital where the governor resided was too close for comfort. If the appointment was confirmed — and the rumor had yet to appear in print — then there was no reason to stay in Tsehchow within reach of such a dangerous man. Perhaps, she hoped, William's conversation with the magistrate would finally shake him out of his complacency.

But it was doubtful. Emily had seen how William's conviction had hardened since his illness; there would be no moving him. After his last meeting at the yamen, William had been obviously annoyed. It seemed there was some question of property rights on which the two men disagreed; and William had come home more determined than ever to dig in his heels. His intransigence with the local officials made her nervous; he was digging himself in so deeply that there would be — could be — no escape.

To Emily, the danger was almost palpable. She saw that the magistrate's objection to William's purchase of the new property was part of a wider scheme of things where every action by the foreigner was detestable to the native — where the native constantly watched for mistakes and slips as ways to bring the foreign devil down. It was hard to understand her own husband's inability to relate this dangerous state of affairs to their present situation. Intuitively, Emily felt that whatever they did, however admirably they conducted themselves, they would be reviled; and when she read, in their stale copy of the *North China Herald*, the increasing number of accounts of attacks on missionaries, her imagination took flight and she stepped right into the bloodied courtyards and the broken houses of the abandoned stations. That the newspaper referred scornfully to the Boxers as "buffoons and rowdies who cavort in pathetic and ineffectual ritual of menace" was small comfort; the writers lobbed their remarks from the safety of the coast.

Emily heard her husband's step outside on the veranda where James was playing.

"Well, James. So you need a sword now, I see. Is that to defend us?"

"No. It's for killing."

"For killing? And what are you going to kill? Dragons?"

Emily's voice interrupted them. She called from the study, with her usual lack of ceremony, "Is Yü Hsien to be governor?"

"I'll be with you in a moment, my love," said William heavily. He went to the bedroom.

Emily followed him there and waited for her answer.

"He is. But we both knew that, didn't we? However, yes, it's confirmed."

"Then the outlook for the mission is not good."

"Oh, I wouldn't say 'not —' "

"I would. I'd say not at all good. I'd say very, very bad, dreadful in fact. Yü Hsien, a governor who favors the brigands, the men who murder our Christian brothers —"

"Brother."

"Ah, our Christian *brother*. Then I must beg your pardon; and I must remember to tell the Reverend Brooks in my prayers tonight that his murder, being a single case, is acceptable after all."

"Emily!" William turned from the wardrobe angrily.

"I'm sorry. That was uncalled for. But you're so complacent."

"No, not complacent. But I refuse to be afraid. The presence of Yü Hsien in T'ai-yüan is neither here nor there to me. But what does concern me is your attitude. It won't do you any good, getting yourself all worked up. In your condition." William closed the wardrobe door and, dressed now in the trousers, shirt and waistcoat that he always wore under the Chinese gown, he started back for the study. "If you don't feel safe here, we can arrange for your removal."

Emily followed him into the study. He seemed to be finally admitting some danger.

"For *my* removal?"

"With James, of course."

"But without you?"

"I've told you, my dear, I see no reason to leave."

"Then you think Wu's sympathetic? What happened about the Tung ssu Street property?"

"He was friendly."

"But what *happened*?"

"He's asking for us to move. I can see his point of view," William continued, when he saw Emily about to protest. "It's in our own interests, you know. No sense in riling the locals if there's going to be trouble — *if* there is."

"I see. I'm to leave because it's not safe. You're staying because it's safe. But you're moving the chapel because there's going to be trouble . . ." William didn't answer. "When shall you begin all these arrangements?"

"Not until I get Miss Coleridge down from her mountaintop."

"What are you saying?"

William began to collect up some of the papers from the desk. He answered Emily with an unpleasant deliberation in his voice. "That I'm going, my dear, tomorrow, whether or not you have anything to say about it, to advise Miss Coleridge to come down to a more secure place of habitation."

Emily said nothing, expecting William to look up from the

94

desk to catch her expression as she digested his reply. He did not. She took a quick step towards him and struck the papers from his hand, sweeping the rest from the desk.

Thoroughly shocked, William didn't move. After the quarrel in March he was only too well prepared to meet with some resistance; but vehement objections were one thing: this embarrassingly naked emotion quite another. He had suspected his wife of nursing a petty jealousy against Martha, a venial indulgence, something she liked to dwell on. Nothing as intense as this.

She shouted at him. "And leave us here again?"

"Emily! Emily! I don't know what's upsetting you but whatever it is, control yourself. It's not worth it. In your condition."

Emily bent down, ashamed of her outburst, and began awkwardly picking up the papers, trying not to let the tears come. She spoke more quietly.

"You still haven't explained yourself. To us there is no danger; the mission must go on as if nothing unusual were happening. But Martha, Martha is in dire peril and must be rescued at once. What's going on? Make yourself plain, William."

"I can't. Not to you, Emily. Whatever I say, you twist it about. You impute the opposite to all my words. I can't make myself plain to you. You'll have to learn to hear what I'm saying and not what you imagine. The conversation is at an end."

While she was still bewildered about his plans one thing was becoming clear to Emily: William was finally awake to the danger. Clearly the survival of the mission was his first concern, above the safety of his family — though not perhaps above Martha's safety. It made no difference to her that he had duty on his side; and as for faith, in these circumstances it was beginning to seem childlike, perhaps even foolhardy.

Their conversation, as William miscalled it, was taken up again that night. It bore the force of all their recriminations, self-doubts and suspicions, but articulated none. And still William and Emily refused to show each other their true

95

colors. On the visit to Martha, however, they reached a compromise. William acceded to Emily's request. He agreed not to visit Martha personally but instead to send a note insisting on her attendance on them in Tsehchow.

May 14, 1900, Jun-ch'eng

The village was quiet in the heat. Those who could stayed in the shadows. Those who had no work slept. Martha covered her head with a square of silk tied under a straw hat and walked out, as she did every day, to the high bank of rubble that was the southern wall of the village. She climbed the mounds of brick lying loosely in the dry earth and stood squinting against the sunlight.

The land itself seemed to be disintegrating, the bare rock fragmenting in the heat. To Martha's right stood a temple built out above the wall and jutting into the hazy air. No one used it. Whatever tile or lattice could be reached had been removed from its lower tier. The tiles of the upper roof lifted and cracked under the damage of the nesting swifts and everywhere straw and roots poked from the crevices. The stone steps were hidden under a tangle of thorn bushes, brown now in the sun.

Below the wall were scattered houses that clung to the mountain like outcasts, their roofs twisted and warped, their walls leaning, shored up against the plunge of rock. Everywhere the mountain seemed ready to split apart under the awesome pressure of its own mass. The walls and paths from its rubble disappeared again into the same rock and that rock lay everywhere randomly, boulders and giant shards precariously lodged and ready to slip again.

The broken forms had no disquieting effect on Martha, rather she seemed to find a sense of harmony in them. She looked out across the sand-colored rock and on towards the purple peaks and on still into the white distance. Her gaze rested a moment at the great rift, only an empty haze but where she knew the north-south pass to lie, where Tsehchow lay — where William was. She paused there, not searching, not watching, resting only, her lids softly closing, sliding over her sight like a lizard's.

Every day for a month she had come to the wall and every day the distance between herself and the pass had widened. The first time she had gone there to the edge of the village had been on a bright day in April with a dry wind blowing hard. It was the day she had risen with her eyes burning and her hands shaking — from lack of sleep, she imagined — as she rinsed out the empty bottles of restorative and swallowed the dregs.

So she went, running, anxious for the sight of William, hoping to see a clumsy figure approaching along the track that crested the ridge to the east of the wall. Standing there, that first day, she imagined their meeting, how William would chide her, urge her again to return and then how, in an effort to redeem his lack of success, he would reach into his bag and draw out and offer her, offer her the sweet, sweet milk of comfort, the morphine that she craved.

But he did not come. She waited till the shadows lengthened and then she went back, running again to keep her mind from the morphine, running through the streets to her house, catching up a small sheaf of tracts and going out again, blindly, wildly, repeating, "Jesus loves us. Jesus loves us," to fight down the craving.

The next day, William's note arrived.

Tsehchow
April 15, 1900

Dear Miss Coleridge,
    I trust this brief note will find you in sound health and spirit strong and willing to undertake the short journey to our city. Without wishing to alarm you or to give you cause for undue anxiety, I feel it is my duty to advise you of the substance underlying certain of the rumors now

97

current concerning the imminent transference of power in this province. Your position as an unmarried lady is, as you are only too well aware, a particularly vulnerable one. I urge you, therefore, to leave Jun-ch'eng at your earliest possible convenience and, in the company of a servant of whose trustworthiness you can be sure, make your way to Tsehchow where you will be wise to remain until such time as the friendly intentions of the new governor shall become clear.

Mrs. Bancroft and I pray for your safe arrival (by Thursday at the latest) and trust we shall soon be able to give thanks again together.

Your true friend in Christ's work,
William Bancroft

The boy who brought the note watched perplexed as the foreign woman read. She shook her head fiercely as if a fly were buzzing there and she made a motion to put the note down but again and again she brought it back before her eyes. The boy believed then all the tales he had heard and ran frightened from the house carrying no reply to William.

Martha, the note in her hand and its words committed to memory, went out to the wall again, the panting of her breath turning to sobs in her effort to climb the loose bricks. She hoped for a miracle, a mistake, anything to make William come. But again he did not and she stood shivering in the warm, dry wind.

That night she lay trembling and sick by the door of her room until Tang found her there crumpled and wet the next morning. He lifted her gently onto the bed, wiped the mucus and spittle from her face and covered her with the winter sheepskin. Then he withdrew to the kitchen and, taking from round his neck his green phial of opium, prepared a lamp for her and carried it with the pipe into her room. The sweet and sickly fumes curled into the early sunshine. While Tang held the pipe to her lips, Martha sucked and choked and sucked again. She vomited repeatedly into a bowl she clutched beneath her chin, but when it was over she knelt opposite Tang on the rush mat beside the bed and they drank tea together, smiling, not speaking.

Tang came again in the evening and then every evening after that to share his precious tar with her. Then Martha would sleep well and rise early to her mission business, going first to the street stall that served as her chapel and flinging back the rickety shutters to pray there publicly, to thank God for the new day. Each afternoon, her visits and her noon preaching over, Martha would find time in the hot still hour to walk out to the wall; what had begun as an act of despair was transformed into a quiet ritual, the violent cry diminishing to a cloistered chant until she no longer called to William, did not look for him. She was content. One evening she unlocked her writing case, filled the silver inkstand and wrote to William. It was not difficult.

Jun-ch'eng
April 29, 1900

Dear Dr. Bancroft,
Your note to me was so kind. That you should be concerned for my safety is truly a comfort.
You must think me ungrateful for leaving your note unanswered but you should know that I have not been well. The sleeping draught you gave me has had a most unpleasant effect. Dr. Bancroft, it may sound unlikely but I believe it began to exert an unnatural influence on my constitution so that, when the treatment was at an end, my physical condition approached something like starvation.
I tell you this not to alarm you but because, as a physician, you will doubtless understand the implications of these effects and be able to temper the composition of the draught accordingly. Its peculiar power over my own person seems to have dissipated. I am, as one might say after a sickness, on the road to complete recovery.
When you have read this note, Dr. Bancroft, I think

you will understand that for now my dearest wish is to remain here, in isolation from my good friends in Tsehchow, but nevertheless in company of loyal friends at Jun-ch'eng. I believe my health here will find the sanctuary necessary for complete restoration.

I am sincerely grateful for your concern, albeit unfounded, in the other matter. You know my feelings. Once again, I must refuse your kind invitation.

Please do not let Emily know the content of this letter; her imagination is far too vigorous for her own good. I do not want to trouble her.

As ever,
Your true friend,
Martha Coleridge

As soon as the letter was sent (by a boy under strict instructions to deliver it privately and in person to Doctor Bancroft, and Doctor Bancroft only), Martha felt a sense of release from William's mission, from William's life. And afterwards, at the wall in the afternoons, she had been able to look at the rift in the mountains, at the place where William was, and feel only the freedom of the empty air. Her mind had refused to see the damaged contours of her own life, just as her eyes had refused to see the rubble and the wreckage and sought out the peaceful, empty space of oblivion.

Now, turning from the wall, Martha was caught in a sudden vacuum. She did not know where she was, nor what she had to do. Like a traveller walking in a strange room, she was unable to remember how she had come there. The panic subsided when Martha recognized the village again — its familiar stone, its known smells, its fly-pricked heat. Walking back through the streets she was untroubled by the chasm that had opened in her afternoon; it had happened before. She turned her beautiful, blank smile on everyone she passed, serenely oblivious of the response she drew.

There had been changes of attitude among the people of the village but Martha, busy with her own emptiness, had not seen. Once, she had been *K'uang-chieh* for them, the Crazy Sister, a curiosity, a curio, taken up, examined and set aside in the place in their minds reserved for priests and lunatics. For days now their easy indifference had been shifting. Some, while keeping their distance, glared at her rudely; others would not look at all but turned away in deep embarrassment at her unconcern.

Reports had reached her, of course, reports of abuse of fellow missionaries, attacks on them, even reports of government complicity in hostile acts. But the incidents were remote and Martha paid them no special attention, rumors being commonplace and varying only in degrees of ugliness; her present state of consciousness did little to make them more immediate.

She was, therefore, ill-disposed to take Tang seriously when she arrived home and he hurriedly closed the gate behind her.

"T'ai-t'ai! Ah, T'ai-t'ai, you come back safe. Tomorrow I think you stay home. Tang look after you."

"Tang expecting T'ai-t'ai to get sick?"

"Madam listen. Please. Many, many men make plans now to do T'ai-t'ai a great harm."

Martha, thinking he was speaking of the old violation, stopped pretending surprise and without speaking placed her hand gently on his arm, in a sign of gratitude for his concern.

He understood her meaning and shook his head. "No T'ai-t'ai, not that. That is passed. This harm is very great," he spoke now in Mandarin gravely, "so great that you and all your race will die. These men are so many they cover the Middle Kingdom."

"Mr. Tang, I understand what you're saying but I trust my God." Tang opened his mouth to protest, but Martha went on, "There is a danger, yes. I have heard of these men, these Flaming Swords, these Great Swords but we'll talk of them tonight. And we shall pray. Not now, the children will be here any minute."

"T'ai-t'ai, the children are not coming." Tang showed no affected shame at their defection but looked Martha hard in the eyes, hoping to see its significance strike home, hoping

101

she would understand.

"Why ever not? They love your millet cakes more than their fathers fear the Crazy Sister. They always come. Is it the heat? Surely not." Martha had a vague, uneasy feeling, like the dryness in the gullet at the onset of a sickness. Something had gone irreversibly wrong.

Tang's confidence failed him at the last minute. "I make tea now then we talk more."

He went inside, lit the charcoal in the small iron brazier and set a kettle of water to boil. He threw the twigs of tea in the warmed pot and thought about Martha and what was to come. Nothing could stop it now. He checked the tiny bubbles clinging to the insides of the kettle, waiting for exactly the right moment to make his tea. If the dangers did not evaporate, and it was clear they would not, then the Crazy Sister would have to act. She would have either to run away or to kill herself. Carefully he poured the boiling water on the tea then he set the pot aside to brew. He hoped that she would kill herself. He would do much for her but he would not run away from the men of his own village. If she would kill herself he could, with honor, follow. He reached for two small bowls and swiftly, in a long rising motion for each, poured out the tea.

Martha came in and sat down on a low stool, smiling when he handed her the tea. "Don't worry Mr. Tang. I won't be frightened by your bad news. What is it?"

"The children will not come because today is an unlucky day. Everybody knows it. There will be trouble in the great city."

"In Tsehchow?"

"Yes, in Tsehchow. Many men plan to force Wu Hsien to deal with your friends."

"Deal with them?"

"Turn them out of the city."

"No. They'll never go."

"That is what I said — there will be trouble. It will cause much fighting, I am certain."

"Why didn't you tell me this before?"

102

"I learn the news this morning, T'ai-t'ai."

"And they plan to act today?"

"Yes."

"Then we can't warn them."

"No. Your friends bring much danger on themselves. On yourself also. Stay away, stay quiet. Do not show yourself. In a little while the trouble may pass."

"I'll do no such thing. I shall stay here but I'll not stay quiet. I shall pray and I shall do it publicly. The people must learn that we trust God. And when tomorrow they hear — as they must — that Dr. and Mrs. Bancroft are still in Tsehchow and that the mission is still open, then they'll understand that God is truly on our side."

Martha smiled and got up before Tang could answer.

In the market place, she played her part expertly, keeping her mask always in place. Her greatest protection. Had she let it slip, uncovered her shivering apprehension as the crowds began to gather, she would certainly have edged them over into aggression. It was a role she had learned well and today, with her fears closer than ever, her performance was almost perfect. There was a numinous quality to her blank and beautiful gaze, but it had no spiritual source. Before leaving her house, she had drawn slowly on the opium pipe and its sweet smoke had clouded her eyes and kept the world away.

And so Martha held her prayers publicly and no harm came to her. She returned to her house satisfied that the power of prayer would protect her. In her room she sat down and tried to understand the implications of the day's news. Her mind could not hold down the problem. She got out her case again and some yellowed paper and scribbled a note to the Bancrofts to ask them to send word of their safety.

My own position is altogether secure, she wrote. To make quite sure they would not try her again on the subject of withdrawing to the city, she added a few lines about her health, intimating that she feared a return of *the singularly unpleasant condition of a few weeks ago* were she to leave the isolation of Jun-ch'eng.

She folded and sealed the letter and asked Tang to find a

good boy to take it to Tsehchow in the morning. Then she went to the table by the window and, without waiting for Tang, lit the opium lamp for the second time that day.

May 14, 1900, Tsehchow

The night had been hot and noisy. William and Emily had lain awake half the night, listening, drifting in and out of an uneasy sleep, Emily turning often, heavily, trying to find some comfort for her swollen belly. Towards dawn, as she fell soundly asleep with the fatigue of the long night, William quietly got up and dressed. He had many calls outside the city to make, some of them long overdue, some of them newly promised, and chose this early hour for his departure, anxious to leave the city as quickly and discreetly as possible.

William found Chiang about to go out in search of water to buy — it was several days since their well had run dry — and they left the compound together.

The beggars that nightly disrupted the peace had been astir till morning. William saw the signs of looting. He saw, too, the marks of an organized unrest; tattered posters tacked up to door frames. PAO KUO, MIEH YANG — 'Protect the country, destroy the foreigner'; and now some new ones and a subtle change of one character, *Ch'ing*, the dynasty: 'Protect the Ch'ing, destroy the foreigner.' PAO CH'ING, MIEH YANG. PAO CH'ING, MIEH YANG.

William had walked almost half a mile to the rhythm of those words before their significance came home to him; his access to official protection was being undermined. It was as if he were involved in a game of chess where the colors of the pieces switched at random. He found himself placed in direct opposition to the throne, his protector, while the rebels sidled in to safety as its guardians.

At the great crossroads, William stopped Chiang and told him he had changed his plans.

"You go on, Chiang. I'm not taking the North Road after all. If anyone should ask for me on your way tell them I shall come tomorrow."

He left no message for Emily, believing he would be back later that day in accordance with his original plan. He said goodbye to Chiang who went on northward with his barrow of empty casks towards the water carrier's shop.

William turned his mule and headed west through the waking city. On an impulse, he was making his way to the Temple of Eternal Snow on the road to Jun-ch'eng. He had turned the problem of the increasing threat to their safety over and over in his mind and, like Emily with her burden, he had not found any relief. The regional mission at Tientsin had not been helpful. The response to William's telegraph had been a short message: *Make independent arrangements.* The mission office sent a letter to follow and in it explained the difficulty of co-ordinating any action on the part of the out-stations. Plans were liable to change at a moment's notice, others were thwarted in mid-execution. The nearest mission station in the field, it went on, was presently empty, the Fitzsimmonds having taken an early furlough and been forced to close temporarily.

There was no one in the city who could help William. It was no good talking to the magistrate any more. As for Emily, she could discuss nothing without emotion; her one thought was to leave; she seemed to have lost all regard for their purpose in China. There was no one else.

The monk, Li-ch'ih, had a reputation for divinely inspired wisdom and for holiness. William believed neither, but for his long experience as an objective observer of events at the foot of the mountain he sought him out.

The road was steep, rising in hundreds upon hundreds of shallow, flagged steps. The mule behaved stubbornly in the heat so that although William had started early he reached the temple only just before noon.

"Of course," said Li-ch'ih, "I've heard the rumors even here in my seclusion. There's no crime, it seems, too atrocious for the predilection of the Jesus people. It's commonly said that

105

your medicines are compounded from the eyes of children spirited away, powders from their bones — no, Doctor, you don't have to defend your name to me. I give these things as much credence as I give your well-known aptitude for poisoning our wells and driving away the rain; no, it's all nonsense, I know that; no one ever lays a charge that can be substantiated in open court. And why not? They can't think of one, not one."

William bowed slightly in acknowledgement. "You are a man of refined sensibilities and wise indeed, but the people of the city believe the rumors and are becoming restless. If they mean to harm us where should we go for help? To the yamen?"

"No. Not at any cost to the yamen. Wu is a good man but he's an ineffectual administrator; he won't be able to help you for much longer. I've seen how the breath from the Forbidden City has been blowing, stronger and stronger over our countryside, bending everything in its path. Wu bends like the rest of them and the chaff of the I Ho Ch'uan swirls about his ears."

"Then if not to the yamen?"

"You'll have to turn away from the city."

"But my wife . . ."

"Your wife can ride, can walk. Stay in Tsehchow and she might not be allowed to live."

"Then we should leave for Tientsin?"

"No. Not Tientsin. That way you'll be walking straight into the belly of the furnace; it's too close to Peking. No, go south. Make for the Yangtze."

"But that must be three thousand li!"

"Perhaps, but most of it in Honan. Once you're out of Shansi you'll be safe. Go south by Mien-ch'ih and draw up your route to pass through Hsiang-ch'eng. I have connections that could help you there. You'll need to find the temple, it's called the Lotus of Dawn, and speak to my friend Chang-ch'ao. Tell him who sent you."

"But three thousand li. I don't know if my wife will be able to make such a journey."

"She has no choice, my friend," said Li-ch'ih quietly. "I'll send to Magistrate Wu and petition him for your safe removal from the city. When I hear, as I shall, that you've gone, then I shall send to Hsiang-ch'eng to advise them of your coming."

The two men talked on for a short while before William took his leave. The priest urged him to wait out the hottest part of the day but William was anxious to start back for the mission. He was grateful for the man's sympathy, however impractical his advice seemed; he couldn't bring himself to believe that such a journey really would be necessary. If the worst came to the worst, then the northeast was surely the obvious direction, the quickest route to the coast.

He saddled his black mule loosely, preparing to walk down the steepest part of the track beside her, and said goodbye.

It was when he found himself crossing a wide stretch of bare, straw-colored scree that William saw the men approaching. He was as vulnerable as a black lizard on sand. He saw them quicken their pace and begin to shout.

William made a quick decision. Mounting the mule he urged it back across the wide slope and to the flagged stairway that led to the temple. None of the men was mounted and it was soon all quiet behind him. He stopped and rested the mule, listening for sounds of pursuit. Presently the mule's ears began to twitch and William felt a current of nervousness run through her. He listened. Hearing their voices distinctly now, he kicked his mount on again and stuck to a hard pace until he reached the temple.

Li-ch'ih had heard him coming and was waiting on the steps between the monstrous, snarling guardians of the doorway. He could see that the doctor was in some trouble and led him through to a small side chamber.

It was not long before the men arrived and began to batter at the main door. When Li-ch'ih opened it to them they pushed their way inside and demanded to see the *yang kuei tze*, the foreign devil. It was obvious to the monk that here were no dangerous sectarians but only beggars, hungry men who spent their time searching for impossibly golden opportunities for gain. He answered that they could have no possible

107

business with the stranger.

But the men, between sighting William and arriving at the temple, had concocted an elaborate case against him and demanded to be heard. The foreign devil was responsible for the lack of rain, they said, and was liable therefore to pay dues ("Double," said the man behind him, "double the regular amount") to the fund for the rain procession. Their spokesman, the tallest and thinnest of them, who looked as if his bones were covered with only a layer of rice paper, looked pleased. A procession had been called for that night and he had come, he said — as official debt collector, added the voice behind him — to exact the fine which would ensure its success.

Li-ch'ih listened with dignified patience and a total absence of attention while the men drew up a detailed account of William's debts. Now that the foreigner had come to him for asylum, he was directly responsible for his safety. No matter how he got rid of the men from under his roof, they were bound to reappear along the road and try their luck again when William started back. He didn't want to send to the city for an escort; this was no time to remind the magistrate that the foreigner in his city was an abiding nuisance; better for the doctor to return privately and not be too demanding of official aid until he was ready to leave the city altogether.

"And so the total sum required of the foreigner is . . .?" He had decided that the simplest solution was to deceive the beggars into taking one route while he sent the doctor round by another.

After a little more argument with his confreres, the spokesman announced the sum to be ten ounces of silver.

Li-ch'ih invited the men to sit down and spoke to them at length. Before he finished, he made it plain that he would celebrate completion of the negotiations — should they agree to his plan, of course — with cake and wine, together with a small payment in token of good faith.

Not one of the men demurred. They left soon afterwards, persuaded that there really was an opportunity to profit from the foreign devil's arrest if only they made a public issue of it at the gates of the city and exacted the fine in full view of the gathering crowds. In that way, Li-ch'ih had convinced them, they would avoid the charge of common brigandage with its dreadful repercussions and would gain only credit — not to mention a sizeable chunk of the silver for themselves.

Li-ch'ih came back to William gloating like an unscrupulous merchant. He explained how the men would be waiting pointlessly at the north gate, how they thought William had been instructed to take that way expressly to avoid them, when in fact he would be entering safely by the west. Li-ch'ih had found out that the procession at least was fact and based his plan on the eagerness of the men to get back to the city without wasting more time on the road; he had added, he said, a little encouragement of his own, a few carefully casual remarks about a foreign devil's powers towards nightfall in open country. Li-ch'ih shook his head, laughing to himself, as he recalled the serious, gullible faces straining forward to catch his every word.

William listened with distaste. He privately regretted the time he had lost in coming back and he told Li-ch'ih that he would rather go on and take his chances on the road. The mule was surefooted on the homeward run and he was all for trusting to the Lord; besides, he was considerably larger than any of the thieves.

Li-ch'ih disagreed. In any event, he insisted, William should wait for an hour or two to let the men get clear away. William, conscious of the huge weight of inferred discourtesy in his reluctance, finally acquiesced. When he left two hours later it was with a very mixed opinion of the holy man. This man of superior education and intellect had turned out to be just another conniving, slippery Chinaman. That Li-ch'ih saved William's skin — or at least his purse — fed the hungry men, allowed them to retreat without losing face, and even afforded them a harmless diversion for the rest of the day, William could not appreciate. As far as he was concerned, he was stranded, half a day from home, embroiled in a ludicrous charade cooked up by a dissembling monk.

It was already growing dark when William heard sounds on the track ahead of him. He turned quickly aside into the cover of the last of the pines and listened. There was no doubt that there were men up ahead; the fact that more than the usual number of travellers were likely to be out on the road on this procession night was hardly reassuring: William suspected the men of double-crossing the priest and he was not far from suspecting the priest of some kind of treachery himself. He was so certain of betrayal of one kind or another that he decided his safest route lay neither to the north gate nor to the western approach but to the south.

Risking the lack of a proper track, he dismounted again and cut off down the slope to the right of the track. He made his way with much difficulty in the darkness and did not reach the southern approach to the city, the great trading route, until a further three hours had elapsed.

Although it was past midnight, the gates were open; a few stragglers were still about, making their way out of the city. William welcomed the sight of them, their presence making his own less remarkable. He entered the city without incident and rode quickly to the mission compound, planning to snatch an hour or two of sleep and be awake early next day to make preparations for a prompt and unconditional removal from Tsehchow.

After only a few hours sleep Emily was wakened by a massive contraction. She lay on her side and spread her fingers over the catgut tension of her belly. There was a moment of perfect balance as the baby inside arched to meet the crushing pressure of the womb. Then, gently, gently the muscles slid back to their former state.

Only half past six. Emily was disappointed to be awake again so early. The contraction meant nothing to her. Though her confinement was still more than a month away, she had often felt the tightening, often submitted to its grip. She enjoyed the idea of the baby inside — flexing its muscles, she thought.

She turned away from the clock and was startled at the sight of the empty pillow beside her. The harsh sounds of the night before scrambled out of her sleeping memory and caught her for a moment in intense, unreasoning panic until they dissolved again into the calm pool of the thin morning air and she remembered that the disturbances had come to nothing. There had been rowdiness in the streets until the early hours, and probably looting, but that was all. Doubtless William was out inspecting the compound for damage.

Emily contented herself with watching the rippled shadow of the bamboo blind across the opposite wall. There was an illusion of movement, instability, created by the blurred shadows of the further leaves, the wisteria on the veranda. These shadows trembled and shifted so that the whole wall was dappled with moving light, like the blade of an oar on the river, like the ceiling at the Cove that caught the refracted light from the sea. Emily, engrossed in the changing brightnesses, scarcely noticed the next contraction.

"Amah! Amah! Where are you?" James's voice carried clearly to Emily from his room next to Lin-sao's. Soon she heard them both in the kitchen where Lin-sao began her cheerful grumbling.

Since the cook's desertion of the household, Lin-sao had been asked to prepare the meals. After a decent show of indignation, she had set to with ill-concealed relish in her new appointment. Every morning now she entered the kitchen loudly bemoaning the ignominy she was forced to suffer, the shame she was bringing to her dead parents. In this way she enjoyed the extra wages of the kitchen without any loss of status. Her cleverness always cheered her up.

The voices intruded on the subtle pleasures of the lights and shadows. Emily got up. She put on a heavy silk wrap and went out onto the veranda. The courtyard was peaceful. Emily would have liked to forget the city that stirred beyond the walls. The noise and ugliness of the previous night seemed to bear no relation to the secluded, paved square.

It was already hot.

As William was nowhere to be seen, Emily walked along to the kitchen door.

"Mama!"

"Good morning, James."

111

"Mama, where is — good morning, Mama — Mama, where is Papa?"

"Just what I was going to ask you, James."

Lin-sao turned from the stove, setting the porridge of millet aside to cool.

"There! That is the last breakfast this amah make in this house. Doctor Bancroft out, T'ai-t'ai. Doctor and Chiang go early to north suburb. Chiang buy water."

"Don't we have any left?"

"Yes, T'ai-t'ai. We have water but Chiang say so little we must save. We must buy water while carrier still sell. When all gone then we still have."

"And the doctor? Did he have to go, too?"

"No. Doctor visit. Doctor say he visit all day."

"I see. Well, don't hurry your breakfast, Lin-sao. We shan't open the dispensary today."

Emily went back to her room and took out her diary as she did every day. She knew when to expect the baby but even so she counted the thirty-five days of waiting left to her. She hoped again to find that her arithmetic was out, that there had been a day when she had forgotten to count, so that the number remaining might be less.

Thirty-five days. In Lin-an she had not minded the waiting, the ripening. She had submitted to it, meekly patient as if it were a holy rite she observed, cradling the new soul inside her, loving its warmth. But not this time, not here. She waited for her baby as the people waited for the rain, with a choking impatience, wanting only to be rid of her burden. To be idle was no luxury, only a frustration. And yet, since the talk of her departure, the mission work had become intolerable. The idea of leaving had lingered in her mind, like a strong figure beckoning, promising, diminishing all other responsibilities.

To fill the morning Emily thought of writing home, but it hardly seemed worth the effort. Too much lay in the balance. There was nothing to read, nothing that interested her anyway; William had sent back the books from Dora's parcel. She dressed as slowly as she could, took a large fan with her out onto the veranda and sat on the shaded side. The courtyard

112

offered little diversion. James was occupied somewhere in the cool of the house with Lin-sao and the dog was lying under the shade of the steps. There were no longer any fowl to watch since some insidious disease had killed the last of them. Even the great glazed pots of geraniums had been removed to the comparative cool of the stables, there being too little water to spare for them.

Emily closed her eyes. She placed her hands gently on her belly and thought how quiet the baby was after its thrusting announcements of the early hours. In a little while she heard Chiang in the outer court returning with the water. She listened to the throaty rush of it emptied into the great stone water butt and she opened her eyes to catch Chiang as he came on through to the kitchen.

"Chiang!" He came over to her and bowed. "Chiang, before you go out again could you spare some of that water for the flowers? It has to rain soon and I'm sure we can keep them alive until then."

"Yes, T'ai-t'ai. But Chiang not go out more. Chiang eat."

"But then you'll go to find Doctor Bancroft won't you? He'll need some help."

"No. Doctor not want Chiang."

"But he had trouble in the north suburb last time. He'll want you with him."

"Doctor not go to north suburb. Doctor leave Chiang at great crossroad."

"Then where has he gone? To the yamen?"

"Not to yamen. Doctor take road for Jun-ch'eng."

It was as if a hand had grasped Emily by the hair, yanked her face out of the warm pool where it was contentedly drowning and pulled it up into the burning air where it was the consciousness and not the drowning that caused the pain.

"I see." The brilliant morning sun was suddenly too bright to bear. Emily closed her eyes again. "Don't forget the flowers, will you?"

"Yes, T'ai-t'ai," said Chiang who remained stubbornly inaccurate in his use of her language.

Emily's consciousness, forced into the bright, burning air,

113

was kept there now by one word. Why? Why had William gone there? A hundred reasons why, but why at a time when they were so short of help? Why at dawn? Why without telling her? Not even a note. And why had William deceived Lin-sao and tried to deceive Chiang? Why say one thing and do another?

She was annoyed at herself for her own equanimity in the early morning. She felt as if she had been made a fool for her innocent enjoyment of a few moments' peace. The old feelings of dissatisfaction and irritation broke out again like a burning rash. There was nothing to relieve them. She could not vent her anger on William, nor spend her energy in work. She could not even shake off the miserable clutchings of resentment by walking out beyond the compound, as she might have done in calmer times. She sat on in her wooden chair and turned and turned the one word over in her mind until it was raw. *Why?*

The sun moved higher, shrinking the strip of shade where she sat. The noise from outside, the shouts and the screeching wheels, rose above its usual raucous level. Emily moved inside. It took her a little while to understand that the noise had, indeed, an abnormal intensity to it and, as if timed to confirm her dawning suspicion, there came a battering of staves against the main gates and the sound of objects, stones or brickbats landing in the outer court.

Emily went out as quickly as she could. "Stay inside!" she said as she went past the kitchen, and then, "Chiang! Come with me." She felt no whisper of fear as she went with her swaying walk to the outer gate. Landing as they did smack into her mood of anger and frustration, the brickbats served only to provoke her to action.

"Open the gate quickly!" she hissed at Chiang.

Standing with her feet planted wide apart and her great round belly confronting the street, Emily presented herself to the men and boys outside.

They stood poised there on the street, their arms arrested in attack, their hands still clutching the staves and the bricks. The opening of the gate had run exactly counter to their

114

expectations. None had entry in mind as an objective. Now here was one of the foreign devils in the flesh; angry, and, worse, in an obviously and an extremely unclean state. There was a moment of silence before the weapons clattered to the ground and the rabble scattered like marbles in the gutter.

Emily, too, was taken aback. Expecting a confrontation, she had been prepared to deliver a thorough rating. She released her held breath and looked at Chiang and laughed.

They barred the gate. As Emily bent to reach for the spike at the bottom of the gate she was caught by a spasm of pain. She waited for the contraction to pass, saying nothing. Chiang, who had turned to pick up the bits of debris, did not notice anything but as they made their way back to the house Emily drew another sharp breath. She stood perfectly still, breathing strangely and feeling the screwing, downward pressure that this time came with the pain.

Chiang watched her in deep alarm, responsibility falling on him like more brickbats out of the sky. Poor boy, thought Emily. She was in no doubt now about the baby's intentions.

The pain receded. "Go and see," said Emily, taking a long breath, "what all that fuss was about."

Chiang was obviously relieved to escape this new crisis which he found far more disconcerting than the one they had just averted. "Only be quick," she added, hoping to find out what the situation was and have a man, a boy at least, back on the premises before she was wholly incapacitated.

But the next pain, that came as she asked Lin-sao to help her, drove her to her knees and from there the labor careered at its own fierce pace, drawing the baby headlong into the chaos of that summer.

Emily put her hands forward and rested her knuckles on the ground till the pain subsided.

Lin-sao acted quickly, shedding her servant's manners like shabby clothes, moving deftly, without hesitation, to do what was necessary. She lit the fire under the iron kettle and led James away to his room. Emily heard her turn the lock as she closed him in then she felt Lin-sao's strong arms lifting her onto her feet, helping her to her room, but the pains now

115

were coming in a thunderous storm and before one was finished the next would overwhelm it, carrying Emily deeper and deeper and deeper into the darkness of her own body.

At the high iron bed Emily again sank to her knees as if the wave of pain were solid and had dealt a blow to her legs. She pressed her face to the mattress to stifle the hoarse voice that cried in her throat. Lin-sao could not lift her. She hurried back to the kitchen, found the knife and the cloths and the twine.

Alone now in a flood of pain, Emily might have lost her hold on consciousness but for what happened next. It had seemed to her as if the head of the baby were expanding, expanding against something inside her that would not give but then suddenly it was free and she knew that in another moment the baby's head would slip out into the air somewhere beneath the skirts that still clung heavily about her legs.

"*Saooo!*" Her voice was an unearthly wail as she struggled to change her position and Lin-sao came running in time to throw back the sodden skirts and catch the tiny baby as it slid, tight in its caul, into the world under the amazed eyes of the two women.

The traces of pain had vanished, melted like a footprint in wet sand. Emily lay in a clean shift with the baby asleep at her breast. Already she loved her daughter more than her husband. Her need washed away with the pain. She had no use for him.

James stood beside the bed, his torrent of screaming run out now into a huge, still pool of embarrassment before the baby.

Emily thought about the baby's wild tumble into the world. She thought about Lin-sao bending to take the baby's head in the palms of her hands, of her two thumbs rubbing away the shrinking mask of membrane, of her lips beaded with sweat, covering the stone gray flesh of the face and blowing, blowing gently over its nose and mouth until the first bubbling cry escaped. She thought of Lin-sao intoning her heathen prayer, "Stay away, stay away," as she cut the cord and bound it. She smiled to remember Lin-sao looking round after she made the cut, looking for her devils, she supposed, flying in at the doorway.

Emily offered her prayers of thanks.

In her own room, Lin-sao succumbed to the fear that had settled on her at the sight of the caul. The baby would die. She knew the baby would die. And the doctor would return. She closed the shutters against him.

"Stay away, stay away." She repeated the phrase like an incantation as she searched for her incense. For the first time since Edward's death, she lit the wands and her hands trembled. "Stay away, stay away, stay away," she moaned, dreading to see William's black-browed face appear in her doorway. She drew the caul from her sleeve, placed it between the wands of incense and bowed. And then she prayed with every bone in her body to Kuan Yin, to the Goddess of Mercy, to let the baby live.

James still had nothing to say to the white-clothed forms of his mother and his sister. Emily took pity on his aloneness.

"Look," she said. "Look at her tiny hands." She pulled a minute clenched fist from the linen and James smiled. Again Emily thought of Lin-sao's great, gentle hands cupping the stone gray face and she remembered those same hands in another season lighting the forbidden incense for Edward.

"We shall call her Mercy," she said to James.

When Chiang came back, hot and worried, he listened to the news of the birth without surprise and then he reported to Lin-sao what he had learned in the city.

There was new trouble. The magistrate had announced that a procession must take place that evening to pray for rain. Some of the people, Chiang said, took this as proof that the *hsien-ling* was actually protecting the mission. They had had a riot planned to break out at the mission that night and had hoped to attract half the city to it to drive away the foreigners, the whole household, and appease the heavens. Now some of them were more angry than ever, believing their plot to be discovered. They said Wu had called the procession only to thwart them and that such a purpose would so incense the

117

gods that the rain would not come at all.

Lin-sao sat quietly with her hands in her lap. She felt a sudden, altogether different fear, a feeling as if a wave rocked the blood in her veins. She looked directly at Chiang.

"We're in danger, aren't we?"

Chiang nodded. "But we must not be afraid," he said. "Remember the doctor's words, 'God is our Father, Jesus is our brother.' Think of them. We belong to them now. These are gods more powerful than ten thousand angry men." He patted her hands and smiled. "The doctor will be back soon. Nothing can happen to us."

"Save your bad news for the doctor," said Lin-sao. "We shall not trouble the T'ai-t'ai."

Chiang agreed that it was best.

None of the other workers came to the mission that day and Emily, Chiang and Lin-sao were, each for their own reasons, trapped there. The heat laid siege to the walled compound. After midday, the baked bricks gave off their heat into the air so there was no cooling. In Emily's room, the shadows on the wall did not move, the leaves outside hung limply on the vine, but a shimmering smoked over the shadows, the haze of the heat itself. The very stones were breathing heat.

James, who had begun killing flies and quickly exhausted the novelty of the challenge, rolled about in a torment of boredom, kicking aimlessly at the legs of the chairs on the veranda. Lin-sao, sweating profusely, worked on at her usual tasks, trying to keep her mind on the narrow track of duty that ran straight as a railroad between her fears. Chiang thought the night might bring yet more serious threats to them, and he slept.

Outside, the city was noisy, perhaps more noisy than usual; Emily supposed it was the complete quiet of the compound that made it seem so. She accepted Lin-sao's confused report that the morning's disturbance had been caused by the stragglers from a mob following a criminal's cage to the western wall. She did not really care, stroking the black down that grew on the baby's brow. The child was unfinished, unready. Emily was glad that William was not there to hold the infant in its raw, waxy newness. She was glad to have her daughter to herself.

Sometimes the thought of William and Martha returned like a pain she had been trying to forget. If he was with Martha, if that was what he wanted, she was glad; he wouldn't be back before tomorrow — the child was all hers. For the pleasure of seeing a flicker of consciousness pass over the baby's sleeping face, she gently moved her, concentrating on forgetting.

By evening the heat had scarcely abated. No air circulated inside the walls of the mission. The noise from outside, as if fueled by the heat, showed no signs of dying down with the day. Lin-sao had moved the baby to her cradle in an effort to cool the mother. She changed the damp bedding often. James said he couldn't sleep. He sat outside with Chiang and listened to the crickets he kept in tiny cages beside the steps.

It became impossible to ignore the commotion outside. There was no doubt that people were again gathering in the streets. Emily asked Lin-sao to bring Chiang to her and heard him tell again, in his own words, what had caused the morning's disturbance. She listened and this time she did not believe him. He waited for the next question, knowing what it would be.

"And so what's all this noise in the streets that we can hear now, this disorder?"

"No disorder. Only procession the people make ready. There is always procession at this time to pray for rain."

"I see. Then we shall pray too," said Emily. She made Chiang wait outside while Lin-sao helped her out of bed and into her wrap and then she stood between her servants, with James in front of her. In a long prayer, spoken in slow, careful Mandarin, she begged God to send rain to the suffering people of the district and then, in English, she briefly pronounced her act of faith that the Lord would provide, as He had done before, the protection that they, the household, needed.

When she had finished, she asked Lin-sao and Chiang to fetch their Bibles and watch with her. Lin-sao sat, with James

119

dozing at her feet, by Mercy's cradle, struggling to make out the characters in her Bible. Chiang lay outside the door, resting his head on the thick book as he did each night.

Emily had made all the provision she could for whatever the night held in store. The elation of the morning had gradually receded in the wake of the pain. The baby sleeping now apart from her, a separate being, Emily was again housekeeper and mother to a strange collection of dependents. Her consciousness of the city returned more strongly than ever and walled her in with its squalor and noise.

She began to chafe again at the idea of William's absence that a few hours before, with her daughter by her side, was easy to forgive. He knew how far advanced her confinement was — it was thoughtless of him to leave her. That he did so in a time of drought, when the people seemed duty-bound to behave like savages, was dangerous and selfish in the extreme; but that he left her, albeit for only one day, without a word of explanation, without even leaving her a note . . . In Emily's imagination, William achieved a degree of flintiness and cowardice that he never could have matched in the flesh.

The room grew stale and stifling. The tension of waiting did not break until after ten o'clock when Emily and Lin-sao finally heard the gongs that signalled the start of the procession. The sounds of shouting and banging came to them in waves, each higher and closer than the one before.

Outside, at each of the compound gates, yamen guards stood, sent by the magistrate to deflect the anger of the crowd back into itself and on to the final, purging climax at the temple. He had not troubled to send word to the mission; the guards were a political necessity, not a courtesy.

The main body of the procession drew level with the mission building. The dog at the gate ran backwards and forwards, snapping at the base of it in its frustration. Chiang was up now, standing with his back to Emily's door. James pleaded to be allowed to go out and watch the dragon. "There is no dragon," said Emily. "There is only the devil." She pulled him up into the bed and began to read aloud to him:

120

"Ask ye of the Lord rain
in the time of the latter rain
so the Lord shall make bright clouds,
and give them showers of rain,
to every one grass in the field."

The noise had reached a crescendo. Lin-sao closed her book and made to kneel. "Go on reading," said Emily. "There is no need to pray again. We have asked God for help. It is enough. We are in His hands." She delivered each phrase like a blow, a shove, until Lin-sao was back in her chair.

And in that little while the procession had passed, rounded the corner, leaving only the echoes of shouts behind it. "Now we shall pray," said Emily, and, from her bed where her trembling might not be noticed, she bowed her head and gave thanks.

May 15, 1900, Tsehchow

It came as no surprise to William, when he arrived home in the early hours of the morning, that Chiang was already at the gate, anxious to let him in. Naturally they would have been worried — all of them. He could imagine how they must have watched for him through the night, hourly more fearful for his safety. The assumption Chiang had made — and unwittingly put about — that he had set out for Jun-ch'eng and had spent the night in relative comfort there, did not occur to William, and he expected to be met with nothing other than relief on his return.

He had difficulty understanding the news Chiang whispered urgently to him the moment he was inside the gate. "Madam has done what?" he said, not believing. Chiang repeated what Madam had done and the scenery in William's careful tableau collapsed around him.

"She can't have. . ."

121

Chiang was suddenly old, looking patiently at a petulant child. He waited for the news to drop through the surface of resistance.

William couldn't think clearly. He knew only that he didn't want it to be. He grasped for a conventional response, a familiar handhold, like a blind man in a building nudged by an earthquake.

"Is Madam well? And the baby . . . my daughter? Are they both well?" He told Chiang that he would go first to pray before he went to Mrs. Bancroft. Chiang lit the lamps in the chapel for him and William knelt there, thinking.

His experiences on the road had confirmed that the time had come for them, all of them, to leave. Now all his plans were upset; it was out of the question for Emily to travel; they were trapped. He wondered how much he should tell her. He didn't want to tell her what had happened to him on the road and frighten her, perhaps unnecessarily; it might be just as well if she didn't even know he'd been to see Li-ch'ih. It seemed especially cruel to discuss any of it while she was still lying weak in her bed.

Instead, he decided, he would prepare Chiang and the amah for the family's imminent departure and make ready in secret. He could engage a large cart and muleteers to leave on notice, have a quantity of silver weighed and marked and have provisions and clothes ready to go. Then, as soon as he saw signs that Emily and the baby might be fit to travel, they would leave under the auspices of official protection from the yamen.

William bowed his head and thanked God for directing him on a true and safe course. In front of the kitchen, he drew a little water from the urn and washed the dust from his face before he went to Emily, who lay in her room, sleeping thinly through the remnants of the restless night.

She was confused when she opened her eyes to find William beside the bed. "William! I thought . . ." Emily saw the image, the familiar fantasy, of William and Martha reaching out hands to greet each other.

"No, my love," said William. "I'm safe."

She looked at him questioningly.

"Is that so hard to believe?" he asked. "But let me see the little one. Where is she?"

Emily gestured to the cradle, a small frown round her eyes. She watched William coldly as he took the lamp and bent over her baby. His clothes were filthy and he smelled strongly of sweat. He must have ridden like a wild thing. There and back. For the sake of a few hours. She didn't want him to pick up the baby.

William looked at the child with a disturbing mixture of love for a thing of his own and rejection of a thing hastily completed. His daughter's face was minute and wrinkled, like the face of any newborn infant, but her eyes bulged under pale, creased lids like those of a bird just out of the shell and across her brow was a dark, simian down.

"Too soon," he whispered and turned, startled, as he heard Emily behind him climbing from the bed. He protested and tried to make her lie still but she was out and pushing past him, picking up the baby deftly and standing with it held tight to her, like a tiny monkey high against her shoulder. Despite his dutiful objections, William was gratified to see how strong his wife was.

"Where have you been?" said Emily.

To William it sounded more like a challenge than a wife's loving concern. "Oh, I'm sorry," he said. "You shouldn't have worried yourself; it wasn't necessary. I went to the south suburb," he added, thinking of his re-entry to the city and forgetting that Chiang would have known he'd taken the west road. "So much to do there, you know. It got later and later until in the end I had no choice. Had to stay put 'til after the procession. You weren't too alarmed, I hope?"

"No. We weren't alarmed," said Emily, laying the baby in the bed. She too climbed in. "You must be tired," she said. "Lin-sao can make up a cot for you in Jamie's room." She eased herself under the thin cotton cover and turned away towards the baby.

"You can put out the lamp," she said.

William paused only a moment before he left. He went to

Lin-sao's room and listened. She was sleeping soundly. He made a cot for himself on the veranda and lay down. He waited until the entire household was asleep and then he went to his study. In the growing light, he began to pack his personal effects, collecting the papers he would need and drawing up the documents that would procure him sufficient silver for the journey. He went to each room, quietly collecting essential items: medical supplies, a few cooking utensils and water vessels, knives and tools, clothes and some valuables.

By the time the sounds of the town began to filter again into the compound, William had two boxes packed and stowed away in the stable. But the day of the fifteenth dawned clear with an unfamiliar freshness and within an hour clouds rolled up from the west and drenched all the country round with heavy rain. In a little while the city had emptied and cleared its choked streets as the people went eagerly to the fields to help in the sowing.

The magistrate in his yamen, the monks in their temples and the foreign devils in their mission gave thanks that their prayers were answered. When Wu's prayers were finished, he set about trying to consolidate the sudden vulnerable peace that had arrived in his city. He had the previous morning's rioters rounded up and beaten and two of their leaders placed in the cangue. The men were, he suspected, members of a sect less malleable than the I Ho Ch'uan, but this was a suspicion he kept strictly to himself. On the official proclamation of their crimes, he listed trespass, mischief, injury to property, interference in relations with foreign powers and violation of the ancient code of hospitality. He thought over the wording carefully. He did not want to encourage trouble; the example should serve to stem it; if, on the other hand, his fractious subjects were still restless, he wanted to be sure that he had clearly directed them to the proper object of their discontent.

For now the people smiled and rejoiced in a new hope for the second planting. The rain had settled the dust of the procession and sweetened the air; it ran through the streets in brown channels where children stood squeezing the mud with their toes.

As the day wore on, William became convinced that the crisis had passed. He took the precaution of having his silver weighed out anyway, but he put the rest of his plan aside. The violence of this drought season had surpassed that of any other. He had worried that departure would be forced upon them at exactly the moment when they would be least able to face a journey. Now the rain had changed everything; the city had returned to its unnoticing, undemanding, long-suffering self.

Later in the afternoon, William heard a small disturbance. When he looked out from the gate and saw two figures driven along by a few men through the empty streets, shambling under heavy cangues, he felt strongly comforted. And when he read the notices pasted on those giant wooden collars he went inside and gave thanks that the Lord had been pleased to deliver him from his trouble — and that the city official had miraculously proved himself on the side of righteousness after all.

He began to associate the new infant with the rain that had cleared the air, a sign of life — no matter how tenuous — a renewal. He felt a desire to make amends for his coldness and he tried in his awkward way to move closer to Emily and Mercy. But Emily was no longer amenable to such tiresome shifts of inclination. She had closed herself around the tiny baby as if she would have her inside herself again. When William spoke, Emily answered but looked only at the dark head of the baby. William's hands reached to touch his daughter but his wife put out her own hand, took his, keeping them off the baby, holding them without warmth, under sufferance, as if she were offering herself, a sacrifice, in defense of the child.

Early in the evening, tired of his balked attempts to befriend his only friend, William kissed Emily on the forehead and went out to the courtyard to stand in the cool washed air.

Emily, who had lain in bed all day, got up and looked out between the slats of the blind which was still drawn down. The yard was all changed. It glowed with color, the wet brick reflecting the purple sky. William stood, hands tucked into

125

his gown, looking at branches of the fig, looking at the patterns. Paper silhouettes against the sky, thought Emily, remembering the black branches.

William was not alone for long. As Emily watched, Chiang strode across the courtyard with a ragged-looking boy trotting behind him. Milking his moment of power, Chiang made an elaborate gesture and received a folded paper from the boy which he handed on open palms to William before cuffing the messenger out of sight again. In the big bed, Mercy began to cry. Emily did not go to her; instead, she watched as William slowly read the letter, then folded it and put it in the side pocket of his gown.

Emily climbed into bed quickly and picked up the crying baby, waiting for William to come in with the news. She saw his dark shape pass the blind and go on towards the study. Her thoughts flew to Jun-ch'eng. When Lin-sao came to her with her warmed canned milk, Emily asked her questions skilfully.

"Chiang had a very important visitor, I see."

"No, T'ai-t'ai, only poor runner."

"Oh, a yamen runner."

"No, T'ai-t'ai. Jun-ch'eng boy." Lin-sao retreated to her own language to pass her judgement of the Jun-ch'eng people: "You should have heard him. He could hardly put two words together. Those mountain people are pigs of ignorance." She looked at Emily who made no comment. "But amah say bad thing," she said, in pidgin again. "Mountain people work hard. Amah not wish to say bad thing."

Emily, her suspicions confirmed, was not listening. William might have rescued her: a word, openly, about the letter might have been enough — just might have been . . . When he came again to the bedroom, not to talk but early to sleep beside his wife, he found her lying with Mercy cradled in the crook of her arm. She smiled thinly at him and asked him not to leave James alone just yet, not until the fright of the previous evening was well out of the way.

"Sleep in James's room, won't you?" she said. "If you wouldn't mind."

126

As Emily had expected, William replied to Martha's letter. He told her that they were by the grace of God safe, and then he gave her the unexpected news of the birth of his daughter. To Martha's own situation, he made little reference, sure that she was over the worst, but reluctant, after her dramatic hints, to have her with them in the city. If she were still making distasteful allusions to that painful time, then it would be far better for her to stay away now that everything had calmed down. He wished the woman would bury the matter once and for all, as he had done.

And there was something else: he described it to himself as Emily's weakness and the child's fragility, but it was in reality his fragile marriage that was threatened by the bold touch of Martha's friendship. Now that it had been withdrawn, it was the friendship of his own wife that William wanted more than any other.

The brief note was a relief to Martha. She was glad that the danger to the Bancrofts was over — relieved, too, to find no more of the pointless exhortations to join them. As she crumpled the letter, Martha felt something unlock. She could breathe again, let go, do exactly as she wanted — crumble and merge, if it pleased her, like the rest of the precarious village, into the hot stone of the mountain.

The joyful note Martha sent the next day, congratulating the Bancrofts on the birth of the baby, was received by Emily with bitter satisfaction: here was concrete evidence that a secret communication had taken place. Emily's morbid obsession had finally proved unkindly rewarding.

June 1900, Tsehchow

Day after day passed under the flat sky, blank as the gaze of a dead man. The peace left behind by the rain had hardened and become brittle under the sun and it became clear that the single rainfall had been just that, a freak, the spiteful trick of

127

an affronted deity. The seed lay swollen and ready in the earth. Only windblown dust trickled from the chutes and ducts that fed the fields.

In their desperation the people drew water for the seed from their shrinking wells. They carried their chipped and flaking idols out into the fields to witness again the bare earth, the cloudless sky, the pity.

Soon the men stopped pretending and saved their water for themselves. Some of them dug up the seed, shrivelled and dried now, and scattered it at the feet of their gods, scattered their hope. Others took the seed in their hands and asked why the rain did not come and looked towards the big brick building of the mission and threw down the seed in disgust. They petitioned the city officials to turn out the foreigners; their own lives were at stake in the famine that would surely follow the drought.

Then they left a warning. No one knew how it was done. Somehow they got into the mission compound. Somehow they seized the yard dog. No one heard a sound but the next morning the fate of the animal was there for all to see. Lin-sao's screams woke the household. While Emily ran to James's room, William ran outside. In the outer yard he found Lin-sao retching drily into her hands. On the wall hung the severed legs of the mission dog. The head rested with the tail in its mouth.

William shook Lin-sao ferociously. "Think of the boy, woman, think of the boy!"

She stopped retching and shook her head violently, her lips slack and ugly. Chiang, horrified, watched from the gate-room where he had been sleeping. The implications for him were obvious. He had slept through the whole nightmare. He dreaded William's reaction, but more than that he dreaded the significance of the act itself. Deeply superstitious, he was overcome with helplessness. He backed into his room and sat down. Do what he might, William could not force him to approach the remains. He asked Lin-sao to go and tell Emily that it was nothing — that a beggar had broken in, that she had set light to a cloth in the kitchen, anything — then he set to work to remove all trace of what had happened.

The same morning, news reached them of the massacre at Shang-te fu. William made his decision to leave. It was a sign from God, he said, a warning. Emily, numbed by what they had heard, showed no reaction to his sudden decision and did little to help but walked slowly to and fro with Mercy in her arms.

The cart was hired and the muleteers persuaded, with twelve thousand cash, to start that afternoon. William mapped out the route, saying nothing about Li-ch'ih's advice but keeping in mind the sanctuaries he had named. The northeast route was rumored to be ablaze with riots; they would certainly head south, for Hankow and the British gunboats. And they would do it immediately, without the help of magistrate Wu. The missionaries of Shang-te fu, it seemed, had been murdered within the precincts of their yamen.

It was agreed that Martha must without question accompany them. William would ride there on his own black mare, taking Emily's mule for Martha. Chiang, the women and the children would go by cart with the muleteers on the lower road and meet in three days' time at P'u-chang.

William prayed hard about that decision. He knew he was abandoning his wife to the charge of her Chinese escorts, something he had said he would not do, but he saw no other way out. Martha had to be fetched down.

Emily, for her part, did not object in any way to her escort; she was, on the contrary, appalled to learn that William had ordered Chiang to return, directly after the rendezvous at P'u-chang, to look after the mission buildings. She tried to argue for Chiang to accompany them all the way but came up each time against the stone-wall defense that William had constructed for his religious conscience: they were not abandoning the mission or its followers; they would return; it was their *duty* to return, soon, and Chiang was the official advertisement that William was doing the righteous thing, the sign that the promise would be kept.

As always when his pride was at stake, William was immovable. There was nothing, Emily realized, to be done,

129

although she would have gladly taken Chiang all the way to Shanghai — to Halifax had it been necessary. What she did resent, however, was the westward detour imposed on their journey by Martha playing the mad anchoress in her mountain retreat. She thought about it often as the cart rattled and bounced on its crazy descent of the T'ai-hang shan towards P'u-chang and the Yellow River.

What Emily could not have guessed was that the Martha William would find there in Jun-ch'eng would not be far removed from her image of the mad woman.

William reached the remote village in the early hours of the morning. When he knocked at the gate of Martha's house it was not Tang but Martha herself who came to open it, wild-eyed and staring and unable to catch his meaning. William waited in the kitchen, which was next to her room. The whole house was pervaded by the sweet and sickly smell of opium. Tang, who had been asleep, appeared eventually from across the yard and sat staring blearily while William explained that they were leaving. He offered to get ready, but William said there was no need. It was not difficult for him to persuade either of them to do as he wished. They listened to him, staring with blank eyes, agreeing to all his plans as the best of all possible arrangements.

The next day, on their wild scramble down the mountain range towards P'u-chang, Martha began to realize what was happening. It began as a nauseous void in the pit of her stomach and spread sickeningly throughout her body. She stopped in the middle of the track. "Doctor Bancroft," she called, "I'm going back now. Please carry on without me." And she turned her mule.

William wheeled round and caught up with her.

"No, please!" she protested as he caught hold of the halter. Emily's mule began to swerve and kick at the black mare. Martha felt as if the spinning earth had changed direction but she knew she had to hang on and she had to get back. "Please! Please!" she protested again while all the time William's voice thundered above her head, insisting, insisting. Her knuckles had turned white on the reins when William finally in his anger and his desperation to get on down the track raised his fist and knocked her sideways from the mule.

Martha knelt on all fours on the stony track, still pleading. The sight enraged William, who rained down such a storm of invective on her and her sins that she felt as if the sky were slamming down to stifle her and she stopped.

"Now get up," he went on, "and we'll find that mule. You'll get on it, Miss Coleridge, and you'll ride with me, without any further protest. And don't let it slip your mind on one foot of this trail that you are a lost woman, damned to hell, Miss Coleridge, for your sin, until you show me you have renounced it forever."

By the time Martha's need for the drug overwhelmed her a second time, they were far from Jun-ch'eng; a promise of help at the next resting place was enough to induce her to carry on.

As they knelt to pray together to stave off her hunger for the drug, in Jun-ch'eng Tang put down his finished pipe and went out to the yard. He carried a long silken cord and he hanged himself from the rafters that stuck through the thatch.

Martha began to shiver as she rode beside William. At the inn she sat huddled in a corner and jerked spasmodically from time to time. Once she whimpered very low. There was something so unmistakably amiss that no one came near to trouble them.

William watched. Had he risked their safety for this: a sinner, steeped in depravity? Clearly she wasn't worth it. She seemed to be disintegrating before his eyes, and when he saw her slip into that foul state of craving he was not only repulsed but afraid, too. She might never recover even an appearance of well-being before P'u-chang; her condition pointed a trail back to an earlier trail of his own. William wished he could leave her, but fortunately for Martha he could not abandon his self-appointed duty. Perhaps also fortunately, he could not bring himself to keep his word and get her the extract he had promised; no other night after that long watch at the inn was ever to take her again to the bottom of the abyss.

On the final day, William slowed their pace considerably so that their arrival at the inn at P'u-chang was late. After they had greeted the rest of the party, there was time only to roll out the bedding onto the k'ang and lie down. William watched Martha until she dropped into an uneasy sleep. He didn't want her slinking away unobserved. There was a good chance that she would find what she needed outside.

Emily, too, lay awake, staring at the greasy smoke-blackened ceiling and watching the bugs crawl in and out between the bricks of the k'ang. She thought about William and Martha's arrival. It was as if two strangers had entered the room: William theatrically solicitous and affectionate towards her, seeming to want to place himself between Martha and herself; Martha simply staring, absent, not there at all, not Martha. There was something that Emily did not understand, an obstruction in the path of her thought; the wheels of her mind rolled by on either side, missing it completely. But the obstacle remained.

A third figure lay pretending to sleep. Lin-sao was not about to drop into oblivion while the Crazy Sister was conscious. The sight of Martha, tall and silent and staring, had been enough to put the fear of the devil into the amah. Only when she thought Martha was safely asleep did she let herself doze into a half-state. When, in the small hours of the morning, she woke and saw Martha sitting bolt upright, shuddering and twitching like one possessed, she was beside herself with fear. Lin-sao was scared already by the journey in this wild province, but now the prospect of travelling farther into the countryside with the Crazy Sister, the devil woman, as a companion was too much for her. When the others woke up the next morning she was already several hours away. She did not take the Tsehchow road, afraid of being overtaken and stopped by Chiang on his return. Instead she made for Jun-ch'eng, hoping to find Tang there. Tang would help her.

"Where's Lin-sao?" said Emily. No one knew. She asked everyone in sight. No one knew anything about it.

"William, she's just disappeared," she said. "We've got to

132

do something."

William was helping reload the cart. "She's run away," he said. "That's obvious."

"She can't have. There must be something wrong."

"She's let us down, that's what's wrong. And she's not worth another minute of our time."

"But why?"

William kept his answer to himself, thinking of the valuables Lin-sao had helped him stow away in secrecy in Tsehchow.

"She must have been afraid," said Emily. "We've got to find her."

"Get James out here," said William. "We're wasting time."

Emily was devastated. She had lost everything she relied on. Lin-sao was her support. Visions of the amah's tenderness hung in her tears. She tried to accept that Lin-sao's fears of the journey, the Yellow River, the unknown, were greater than her love for the children. At the same time her disappearance seemed to Emily like something expected, or something already dreamed. Martha's coming amongst them as a stranger was an omen. A sense of foreboding hung about the journey and the amah's desertion was the first evidence that luck, or whatever it was, was not with them.

"William," she said when the cart was ready, "I'd like Chiang to come with us, now that we don't have Lin-sao."

"Chiang's going back," said William. "I've already given him orders."

"William, please reconsider," said Emily. "We need someone we can trust —"

"Like Lin-sao?"

"William, we need Chiang. He'll be able to help us."

"I'm perfectly capable of getting us to safety. If you'll just allow us to start. Chiang has his orders and I'm not changing them now."

When William went to find the muleteers, Emily made her last attempt. "Chiang," she said, going up to him where he was saying goodbye to James. "Most loyal and respected Chiang," and out of sight of William she did the unforgivable

133

and bowed low to the servant, nodding her head to her knees. "Please, I beg you to accompany us on our journey."

"Madam," said Chiang, looking very much alarmed. "Master have said return Tsehchow. Chiang is returning now." He caught sight of the look in Emily's eyes. "T'ai-t'ai and children very dear to Chiang but Chiang have orders to go back. And Lin-sao — " he added, "Chiang have to find Lin-sao."

"Well then, I shan't ask again. I hope you find her." Emily reached out and took Chiang's hand.

When William returned, frowning, Chiang helped him settle with the muleteers and hire new men, a surly-looking pair who were reluctant to start, refusing even to harness the mules until double payment had been agreed and a sizeable portion of it laid out in advance. Emily thought the men must have felt the same forebodings; William thought they were grasping racketeers. Only Chiang knew what was holding them up, had heard the rumors that Yü Hsien was about to arrest every last foreigner in his province.

But he could not tell the doctor. Chiang, in his own way superstitious, believed that the telling itself would be enough to make the rumor fact. The Bancrofts and the Crazy Sister weren't far from the Honan border, nothing could stop them now if they got a good start. He added an extra dash from his own money to the advance paid to the muleteers (for although he loved the Bancrofts he had squeezed the doctor well for this new duty of mission caretaker) and he made the men agree to carry on well into Honan once they had crossed the Huang Ho.

What Chiang did not know, however, was that the trouble was not confined to Shansi, but was seething and boiling throughout Honan too. Nor could he have guessed that Yü Hsien's rhetoric against the foreigner was to inflame the people to such soreness that when there was no foreigner at hand they were to vent all their fury on the third-class devil: the convert, the native Christian who was tainted with the pig smell, the pig blood of the missionaries. And when that time came and Chiang realized his danger there was no gunboat on any river to save him.

He helped the party load up and rode with them on Emily's mule out to the south road. There with the Yellow River in sight he said goodbye, waving once before he cut across country towards the tumbling mountains and the Tsehchow road.

Emily watched him with regret and with deep shame. Now that the danger in Tsehchow was acknowledged, could they really be sending him back there? Wasn't he their responsibility since they had marked him a Christian, a friend? Or did William expect him to desert the mission, to shift for himself? Then it was a doubly dishonorable thing. William watched Chiang with his own misgivings, wondering for the first time about some collusion between Lin-sao and the man; he hoped the property would be safe. None, least of all Martha staring blankly at her own inner ache, realized how great would be their need of Chiang as interpreter, arbitrator, guide through the wilds of the Chinese landscape and the freakish climate of its emotions, for the next week was to churn itself out like a great furrow, flinging them across the plains of Honan like debris from the country's mighty upheaval.

Their arrival at the Yellow River was the first indication that their hopes of Honan were an illusion. The crossing place was thick with vagabonds, most of them in league with the boatmen to extort what they could from travellers. William found himself paying, on each side of the river, more than he would pay Chiang for a week. The new muleteers watched in amazement and whispered as William actually produced the absurd sums that were demanded. Emily was sharply conscious of the menace in the insolent, unaverted stares and tried to distract James so that he would not meet their eyes, turning her own away from the two men as if they were a pair of unpredictable dogs. Martha seemed to notice nothing unusual and, unlike Emily, let her gaze fall where it would with equal detachment and with the utter objectivity of a victim of sea-sickness. She looked the men directly in the eyes and her empty stare beat them down.

As the fact of the Bancrofts' wealth seeped into the open,

135

the dangers for them increased. From the river onward they could not pass a village or a town without a band of men to beg the way in with them and beg the way out. At first, William was able to keep them at a distance by dropping copper cash at intervals along the way and when they left Yi-yang the presence of two tattered yamen runners seemed enough to discourage any more serious kind of trouble. But by Ju, where the runners turned back, the storm that had so long held off broke about them. A band of men and boys hurled stones at them as they passed, and the muleteers pulled up the cart sharply and ordered them to get down, saying they would go no farther under such conditions. William blustered and threatened, but was loath to bribe, since by now he recognized the hazards of advertising his silver.

The party had no choice. They loaded William's black mule with what boxes they could and offered the rest of their belongings to anyone who would undertake to get word of their approach to the next headman. But it was useless for them to look for official protection. The muleteers' desertion, they knew, was a signal that they were fair game. They walked now on the hot plains of Honan without Chinese servants, guards, or guides. It was not long before they were stopped again and the mule and the boxes taken from them. That night they slept with beggars — some of whom had robbed them — outside the walls of the town where William had hoped for help. The next two days followed the same pattern: the cart; the mule, the boxes already taken from them, the silver they had tried to hide was next, then their rings and their watches, and finally their clothes.

At Chia-hsien, the magistrate, who had heard conflicting rumors of the approaching travellers, sent out a petty official with a sedan and a contingent of the yamen guard, meager though it was, to offer protection. He had hopes of a squeeze for himself in this affair, just a little to fatten his purse, but when he found the missionaries reduced to nothing more than starving beggars he found himself in a position worse than embarrassing: he had made himself official guardian of a group of tatterdemalion foreigners with not a copper between them.

He could see that he would clearly lose face whether he helped them or not, perhaps especially if he did not. And so, after a sham trial, he carefully staged their removal from the city with all the appurtenances of official protection, to culminate in their mob execution outside his walls. His plan came close to succeeding but although the most frail, the baby Mercy, was lost to the violence of that attack, the rest of the missionaries were destined to walk out of that particular furnace, delivered into the care not of any ethereal angel but of a dusty, saffron-robed, shaven-headed, pagan priest.

The Temple of the Lotus at Dawn stood at the gates of Hsiang-ch'eng. All through the week that led them there, William had prayed, as he had never prayed before, speaking to his God like a frightened child. In the month before, when he had considered a swift escape, he had seen himself leading his son and the three women, Emily, Martha and the nurse, out of the place of danger. He had seen the muleteers and perhaps an extra coolie or two driving them steadily towards safety while they themselves prayed or sang. He had not seen Martha mad with opium, Emily weak with dysentery, blaspheming while a newborn infant died in her arms. He had not seen the three of them on foot like beggars, carrying the boy, hustled in and driven out of cities. And so, reduced to total dependence, he had prayed from an unknown place, far down in his soul; and when at Hsiang-ch'eng he saw how a haven had been granted to them in the cool shadows of the Buddhist temple, he sensed no irony but only believed with the oblivious conviction born of answered prayers.

Sitting by Emily's side, remembering the most shaming humiliations and the deepest fears he had ever known, understanding slowly that they were safe, that his wife was not about to die, William's gratitude warmed to love. There were not enough people for him to love, to support and help. His charity knew no bounds; no sacrifice for the love of God could be too great a demand.

The only trace of William's stony pride was a pebble, a shingle. It stuck in his throat every time he thanked one of the Buddhist brothers for any one of their hundred kindnesses.

He tasted on it something almost bitter, like irony: he the Christian enduring not despite but because of the work of the pagan he had come to save. He remembered with a pang of guilt Lin-sao's frightened face; the man, Tang, pressing his knuckles against his eyes as they left; Chiang turning round, waving, smiling. William felt a sharp need to outlove these gentle monks; it came as an irritation again and again in his conversations with Chang-ch'ao. The pebble would not be dislodged.

Martha, for her part, had undertaken the first half of the journey in a fog of sickness and craving, hardly knowing their danger, not caring what was happening to them. Often it was her half-crazed look that kept the crowds at bay. But when the craving had passed, a deep blackness descended on her as the knowledge of what she had done began to close in around her. William had prayed with her whenever he could but she mouthed the words only to help him, seeing his own need. She felt herself an outcast from his God's world. The evil of her addiction obsessed her and where before she had not cared about her life, now she looked for its end.

Not for Martha the martyr's crown but the black engulfing flames of oblivion.

Part Three

June 1900, Hsiang-ch'eng

There is pressure at my temples close to my eyes. A circular motion. The heavy ache lightens and lifts. I feel the edges of my eyelids cold against each other. I breathe a faintly pungent spice, smoke. Incense. I want to see. I force the skin of my eyelids to roll back. Close again against a throb of color. Flare of brightness. Orange.

"*Pieh cheng yen!*"

The pressure continues. Fingers. Lifting the sick pain. I let go. Let the fingers take it. Give back sleep. I give you pain. Give me sleep.

"*Ho-pa!*"

A man's voice. Speaking Mandarin.

"Now you will drink. The pain is leaving you. Make your body quiet. Let it drink." And the words sounding gently like water lapping. Healing. Porcelain at my lips. Sweet water. Warm sweet rice water in my mouth. Washing me inside. Cleansing the foulness of the drought.

"Now sleep."

The voice again. The voice as sweet as water. It could heal my soul, wash my spirit.

Open my eyes. I see his face. He is smiling. Oh, look at his eyes, Lin-sao's eyes — deep wells of kindness. The wells fill with my own tears. He bows. Patches of seared skin on the crown of his head, like smudges, thumbprints. The marks of Buddha. He looks up and smiles again.

"Now let your eyes sleep also."

I close my eyes and his fingers touch my face again. Giving. Giving sleep. Giving.

James? . . . and William? There, sleeping. And clean new clothes again. William washed and freshly shaved. His hair tied at the back in a stubby queue. The first time ever. James peaceful, well. And I too am well again. I can feel it. Someone is caring for us. The monk?

But Martha, what is wrong with her? Back and forth, back

141

and forth. The pacing again. Prowling. Martha prowls. She turns and turns. She crosses the squares of sunlight that checker the floor. Ah, look at her face when she comes into the light. She jams her teeth together and her eyes are narrow, narrow. She is in pain. Look, her hands go up, she clutches at the back of her neck and bows her head and still she paces. Close your eyes if she looks this way. There. Don't let her see you awake. Watch her. She turns again. She stops at the wall and presses the side of her head and her shoulder to it. Close . . .

"Emily?"

I sigh softly. Asleep. I don't want to talk. I want to watch. I hear a movement from the other side of the room. She has wakened William.

"Is she awake?"

"No, Doctor, but she's better. I'm sure of that." Martha's voice all myrrh again. Open my eyes. See how she stands now. For William. She is another person. She folds her hands meekly in the sleeves of her clean, satin jacket. She stands humbly, placidly. All the agony out of her. Her face all calm, all composed. But look at her eyes. They don't match her voice. Something frantic there still. Drowning.

William is getting up. Close my eyes quickly. Listen. He's coming to me. I feel his breath on my face.

"It looks as if she's slipping back."

"Doctor, she's better."

"Pray God not take her back now."

I should speak but I do not want to talk. Still less to pray.

"Don't say that. She's better. In a little while she'll be awake and you'll be seeing her smile again. Come on now, we should be ready for Chang-ch'ao. Should we pray together for good news from him? Then I'll wake James."

Listen to their prayers. Martha's like a letter written in a false name. I have seen her misery. I have seen her rub her head against the wall in an agony of despair. Not five minutes ago. Yet she calls herself His *faithful, trusting servant*. No, it isn't true. She does not have faith. She trusts only her own power, her own strength. William's prayers are genuine. Pious and weak, he begs for help from a God who has abused him,

142

but at least he believes his own words. I have heard enough.

"Where are we?" My voice sounds from outside of me.

Martha smiles at me while William dribbles nonsense about death's door. Spewing praise now. To God. Why doesn't he speak to *me*?

Martha bringing water. "It's all right, Emily. We're at Hsiang-ch'eng. In good hands." She ignores William's protest as I begin to get up. Instead she tells me to make myself ready. Good news is coming. We may be leaving soon. William is asking me over and over if I am all right.

I go across to James and he rouses as I bend down. Still sleepy, he puts his arms up to my neck but I cannot hold him. I sit down and keep him close until he shakes off his sleep. My one child. My only. Of all the children I have borne ... the ones that might have been, that never were ... and Edward sucked away by a tide of filth, and Mercy letting her life slip between her lips on a breath. And now you, James, you are my one child. My only. We have to live.

"Mama, you're awake."

"Of course I am, my silly."

"But you were sleeping."

"So were you."

"Yes, but you were sleeping so long and talking too."

I laugh with happiness to listen to my child, my silly child again.

"Yes, Mama, really. You were talking. All about stones and stones and piling on stones. And in Chinese too. Who were you talking to?"

William, folding the quilt I was sleeping on, turns round. "Leave your mother, boy. She's tired."

James pretends not to hear. "But who, Mama? You were so out of breath."

"James!"

"I wish I could tell you, my rabbit, but I slept right through it. Go now to Papa while I make myself ready."

A silk curtain divides the room. Behind it stands a great glazed jar but there is no water. Instead, on a raised platform of lacquered wood, porcelain jars of lotions and salves have

143

been set out for us. There is a little water, for politeness' sake only, set out in tiny bowls. Then it has not rained. Beside the jars there is a pile of folded cloths and a small row of soft brushes to remove the dust from our hair, our ears, our eyes. Pieces of braided black silk lie ready to tie our hair. There is even a blade to trim it. Beside the blade is a small bronze bell so that we may call for assistance. No one then fears us here.

"What is this place?"

"The Temple of the Lotus at Dawn." Martha draws back the curtain and looks in. "You really don't remember anything, do you?"

"No." I am looking into a mirror of silver that gives back a wavy reflection, itself no more than a memory. "Only a face that was kind."

Martha comes in, drawing the curtain closed again behind her. "You became unconscious on the road to Hsiang-ch'eng. We really didn't know how we were going to manage. Poor little James was beside himself with the heat. We were trying, your dear William and I, to get you and James out of the roadway in case any more beggars or soldiers came along. That was when we saw the figure coming in our direction, in the distance, you know, walking all alone towards us.

"Oh, Emily," Martha lowers her voice and something of her old, irreverent manner creeps back, "you should have seen William's face. I think he really thought he was seeing the Second Coming, Christ incarnate on the road to Hsiang-ch'eng. He let go of your arm and dropped to his knees staring." She puts on her most pious face and rounds her eyes in mock wonder. "Only then of course he realized his mistake and started muttering about the heat."

"Poor William."

Martha looks at me. She doesn't know whether I am serious or condescending but her eyes are burning with laughter. She continues in her normal voice. "Anyway, the figure drew closer and we saw at once that he was Chinese, a monk in fact, only his orange robe was so dusty that it was the same color as the road. He came up to us and bowed low but he didn't say anything until he'd given us all a drink from his gourd. Oh, Emily, he's the kindest man. He walked all the way to the city and came back within the hour for us with servants and litters. He brought us straight here and has cared for us himself, though there are nuns here too, for the last two days.

"He thinks he can help us get to the Hupei border. He's with the magistrate now."

"And this is Chang-ch'ao?"

"Ah, you must have been waking. Yes, that's his name. He should be back soon with news of his success."

"But William hasn't seen the magistrate?"

"No."

"Then we don't know his feelings towards foreigners."

"No, but Chang-ch'ao carries some weight in this town. The magistrate will listen."

Martha sounds so confident that it makes me want to believe her. Yet I saw her despair. She has masks for all of us.

"I hope you're right."

We leave the little room and join William and James sitting on the floor. William is trying hard to amuse James with half-remembered finger games and rhymes. Now the hate goes out of me. I was wrong. Martha can't love him. He is all alone. He clings to James who cannot cut him away as I have done — as Martha has done.

I sit beside him and lean my head against his shoulder. He doesn't speak but inclines his head to mine. It is all I want.

James looks at us. "Papa said that people cannot grow again when they are buried in the earth. Not like flowers that come up again."

"That's right, my rabbit."

"Well then, I'm glad."

"Why is that, dear?"

"Because if Mercy grew up again we wouldn't be there to look after her."

William's face presses close against my hair but we don't cry. For James's sake we do not cry.

The bowls stand unfilled beside the pot. We have sipped and

sipped at the fragrant tea until we can drink no more. The monks are kind. Their water is rationed but they tell us we must drink to heal our wounded spirits, to wash away the memories of the thirst.

Chang-ch'ao didn't come yesterday. We waited and waited. But they have cared for us. They have fed us so well we are no longer hungry. Now they bring instead lotus seeds and sugared lemons to tempt us. Something of the man I knew in Lin-an has been coaxed back in the sweetness of this place. William seems closer to us all, to the monks even, though he calls them pagans. They tell us we are free to leave but get us to stay within the protection of their walls. We go about in the little courtyard outside. That is when we see the nuns, the only time. Used like servants here, their robes darned and patched in many places. Ancient, ancient women, bent double, raking, raking at the smooth, even, red gravel though it has already been raked today, though it will be raked again tomorrow.

James is happy. He has forgotten what we are waiting for. One of the old women left toys for him — a little pat-ball, five polished stones and some colored braid. He kneels in the shade of the great peach tree that overhangs the wall and he leans on the stone bench where Martha sits. They are trying to make cats' cradles. They laugh like schoolboys.

"Perhaps we can stay here until the trouble is over."

William turns to me from the doorway. "I think not," he says.

"But we're safe here. The Boxers can't last long against the Manchu bannermen. The empress won't stand for it."

"The dowager? She's not doing anything. The silence of accord, that's what that amounts to."

"Well, we'll make her. The British legation has power. And the others, the French, the Germans."

"It takes time, Emily."

"Then we shall wait. In safety."

"No."

"William, why not? We're safe here. Can't you see that?"

"No. We have to get out of Honan as soon as possible. The

146

sooner we reach the Han and the boats, the better, as far as I'm concerned."

"But the monks will keep us safe."

"We're not their responsibility. They're . . . pagans. They've no duty towards us. None."

"*All men between the four seas are brothers* — they say it all the time. Not even a Buddhist teaching. They don't make those distinctions."

"I'm not going to rest our fates with them and that's that. It would be a grave sin to place less trust in our loving Father than we do in these pagans."

"William, you're not —"

Someone is at the door. We do not speak. Martha and James, silent, look up from their game. A servant enters. Yet another tray of tea. He smiles and bows, setting down the tray on a low table. He picks up the cold pot and bows out. Martha sighs and turns back to James.

"Ah, at last," says William, taking from the brass tray some official cards from the district magistrate. They have red borders.

Martha comes inside and we stand round the tray while William inspects the cards.

"One for each of us. This is my name, Pan Yi-sheng."

I want to ask what they are but my throat is closed with sick anticipation. William is not worried.

"Now. Which is — ah, yes, Pan T'ai-t'ai, that's you, my love." I take my card. "Then this is for Miss Coleridge." He hands her the card. "They are our passports, I believe."

"Criminal."

"What did you say, Miss Coleridge?"

"Criminal. I said 'criminal.'"

"I'm sorry, I —"

"*Fan-jen.* Can't you see? It's the character for criminal."

"No, you can't be right, my dear lady. Let me see."

They are arguing. I read, slowly, translating:

147

I, Emily Bancroft, criminal of the fourth degree, am vouchsafed, by the benevolence of the most high magistrate, Fan Feng-shu, right of passage through the district of his jurisdiction in accordance with the agreed terms of reprieve: that I be expelled never to return again. The most high magistrate, his excellency Fan Feng-shu bids all who honor his authority let me pass unmolested from his dominion.

I look up. Martha and William are silent. William has his eyes closed. Martha flings down the document and goes outside. She stands breathing deeply, fighting off the despair.

"Now what about your Chang-ch'ao? A criminal's passport! Is that what he has so kindly arranged for us?"

"Don't speak so unkindly, Emily. I'm sure he did everything he could. But it's just what I was trying to show you: we have to put our trust in the Lord, not in mortal men."

"But you trusted him. You trusted Chang-ch'ao."

"We don't know yet that he's abused that trust."

But he must have. And yet I can't believe the face I saw was dissembling. I did see love. I did. Eyes cannot lie. There must be something wrong.

There is a knock on the door. It opens before we can answer. The servant introduces a young monk. Although his face is more youthful than Chang-ch'ao's, smoother, his expression is harder. He bows just slightly as we gather to greet him. He speaks a trifle too quickly for etiquette.

"I bring you the compliments of Chang-ch'ao. He regrets deeply his absence. He is presently indisposed and unable to attend his new-found friends. He has obtained for you your passports out of this district. They will conduct you safely to the next district. The magistrate there will renew them or otherwise act as he sees fit."

"But . . ."

William grips my arm very tightly, "Excuse me. Emily. Let me speak —"

"They are criminals' passports!"

William and the monk both stare at me as if I have spat at

148

them.

"The gracious ladies will be pleased to retire to the pleasant courtyard that awaits their enjoyment." The monk bows deeply now. No point in trying to speak with him.

"Come, Jamie. Miss Coleridge and I are going to sit outside. Look, there is the fly-catcher you saw in the peach tree."

The heat batters on the tiles, on the bricks out here, but this shade where we sit is deep. We lean our backs against the wall and look up to where the branches of the peach come billowing over. The hard fruit lies under our feet on the baked tiles. The tree is old. Its roots finger the earth deeply but the drought grips them. The tree is shedding its fruit, saving itself. The leaves next. Already limp, their edges rolling in. Then the tree will stand skinned alive in the hot air. But not dead. The rains will come.

William's voice is quiet now but I heard him submitting, complying: "We are sorry Chang-ch'ao is unable to be here but we acknowledge gratefully his honorable assistance and humbly accept the passports he has obtained for us."

But they are not passports. They are death warrants. They throw us on the whims of every malicious, dissembling official we shall meet. Yesterday, William, I could have loved you again. In the sad sweetness of reviving hope I almost loved you. Not now. It is finished. I cannot believe in you. You will not fight. You surrender meekly to the people you despise and call it trust in God, or brotherly love. Well I call it weakness, resignation and cowardice, and I despise you. And I despair. Nothing left now, no help, no more faith. Finished. Empty. Submit if you will, but I shall not stand by you. Not for that. I shall stand on my own strength this time. I shall bear the trials that are coming but I shall never smile at my enemy, never turn the other cheek, and all my mind shall bend to escape, to life, and I shall be ready when the time comes.

They say it is the fourth day of the sixth moon — the last day of June. How long then, since we left Tsehchow? It could be months, years. The sickness has drained me of all the past. Everything begins anew. No — not everything. Not Mercy.

149

If she could . . . oh, if she could. Lin-sao, I am glad you are not with us. Look at James. Thin despite the care. His eyes wide now in anticipation of our start. What do you see, James? Hold his hand tightly. My rabbit. We're going out to the road again. Perhaps to the Han. If we're lucky. Try not to think how it was before. Try not to look ahead.

"Look James! That's our cart. See how kind the people are."

Four yamen runners are bringing the official cart round to the gate of the temple. The mules look old and worn out.

"For us? And all the yellow flags?"

"Yes, James. Isn't it fine." The yellow flags are most definitely for us, imperial yellow, tying our fates to the careening xenophobia of the empress dowager. Look how they advertise our vulnerability, our ultimate fate: OFFICIALLY FORWARDED BY THE CITY OF HSIANG-CH'ENG TO BE DESPATCHED FROM THE PROVINCE OF HONAN WITHOUT RETURN.

James is absurdly cheered and heartened by the pennants, which he cannot read. He scrambles into the cart and we, in our new Chinese suits, climb in after him. One of the monks comes with four quilts and gives them to us for sleeping rolls. Another ties a rush mat onto the bamboo poles that wave from the sides of the cart. It makes a bowed awning to shield us from the sun. The monks are good men. They have been kind. Saved our lives perhaps. Mine certainly. How angry I was yesterday at the passports they gave us. But they tried. They procured this cart, these guards. I do believe they tried.

Yet Chang-ch'ao never did reappear. The shame of a Judas? No, I can't believe that. What does William think? He called them pagans but he has accepted all their help, their gifts. Their money, even, rolled in a belt around his waist. And William kowtowing — that I had never seen before today, never thought I would see. William shedding his principles, like a miser in a famine, spilling his beautiful, golden coins for the tasteless millet that sticks in his craw.

We wave out of the arched opening as the cart begins to move. The monks bow like mechanical toys. Two of the guards run behind, another sits in front and the fourth trots along on foot with a lead rein. Those two behind are just waiting until we are clear of the city before they jump up here — here where we ride with our death warrants.

James needs to get out of the cart. I ask the driver to stop. He curses me and drives on. And all the smoothly polished peace and the beautiful order of the temple starts to crack and craze in my mind and all the memories of the journey there come rushing in. It is all about to happen again.

Coming awake is like stepping from a mirage back into this body. Every part of it clamors for attention: legs, arms, neck, shoulders. It all happens at once, every muscle stiff and sore from the long journey yesterday and my flesh alive, creeping and twitching against the tracks and bites of the bugs in the night. All of it would be bearable save for this fear which has stretched and tensed my skin until it is the merest membrane, a shred that barely covers the million nerves waiting, poised for the pain. I am a skinned fish dropped on sand. Every grain is killing me.

There is nothing in this filthy room to wash with. Last night, the headman of this village — wherever we are — would have none of us, sent us to this hovel. A place for criminals and beggars. The latrine is a hole outside our window.

"Wake up, Jamie."

Look at him. He doesn't feel me shaking him. So tired.

"Wake up."

Putting his arms up to his head, now covering his face, curling down into a ball. Trying to stay asleep. Pick him up. Waking. Put on the new suit from the monks, push the stretching limbs into the thick cotton. He's going to be hot again. But his limbs must be covered. Even with the mat, the sun burns in on us, finds a way. Take him outside to that filthy hole. Flies there already, waiting to crawl on us.

Martha is up and greeting us hoarsely. She goes outside so that William can shake the bugs out of his clothes. I see her from the doorway stretch like a cat. The escort is out there now.

151

I have a little wooden comb and I run it through and through James's hair and pass it to William. Since Hsiang-ch'eng, he looks less oppressed by our hardship. He runs the comb through quickly and hands it back. He begins to roll up the quilts.

"No time to stop for prayer now. We'll be able to pray when we're underway."

"Of course."

"Get James into the cart. I'll go and see about some water."

The guards are wretched, miserable; they don't return my greeting. James steps directly in front of the most surly and, with his child's disbelief that an answer will not be forthcoming, repeats it.

"*Chi-le ma?*"

The guard sidesteps him, pushing him away with the palm of his hand. Only two men now. The other two, the ones that jumped up in the cart with us yesterday stayed only long enough to get to the next town. They were only boys. They sat for a while, nervous, looking at us as if we were lepers. When Martha lifted her voice and began to sing "Jerusalem, my happy home" they jumped down — our fine fellows — and listened to this she-wolf from a safer distance. Guards! They were scared of us. Made off as soon as we reached the next town. Said they were going to buy us some food and never returned. William a fool to give them the money — William who never trusted anybody.

These two are different, the two that stayed. They are older; they laugh at Martha constantly, rudely. Martha should stay inside, but she walks. Yesterday she actually got out and walked in the full sun. No wonder they laugh. She's mad to draw attention to herself. I don't think they're up to any good, these men. Poor things, half-starved all their lives. These are the men who would cut our throats for a few cash. Our guard — what remains of it.

They're laughing again. This time it's Martha carrying the bedding out of the hut. She doesn't care.

"Here, Martha, sit beside me."

"In a moment."

152

She throws in the bedding and walks over to where they are squatting, their backs against a wall, smoking. She says something. They shake their heads again and again. They are no longer laughing.

She comes back. I want to ask her what she said, but William is here and, as he climbs in, the men get up to drive us out.

William passes round the water gourd.

"I'll lead the prayers, Doctor," says Martha.

Through the heat it stares and stares back at the sun. This never ending plain. As huge and blind as the face of God. Oh, God forgive me. We crawl across it. Flies on the face of God. There cannot be any hope. I cannot hope and as long as I cannot hope then there *is* no hope. I sin against the Holy Spirit. Against my very faith. I cannot be a trusting child. I cannot believe. And so I damn us all. For my sin God will brush the crawling flies from His face, I know it. But if I believe that then I *do* believe.

And yet I cannot.

Oh God, help me! I want to pray but the face I pray to is carved from the dead yellow silt of this forsaken plain. I am faithless and I know it. Oh, help me!

Forsaken. Perhaps forsaken and this is not, after all, my sin, to be foundering without a God, but my punishment. For all the other sins. For my sins with William, when we did sin, for my hatred for him now that we do not. For William's sin against me. For William's and Martha's sins. Together. Yes, a punishment, all cast here for our sins, a sign of a just God, a sign then, of hope. But James? James has not sinned; why should he be punished? And Mercy? Then an unjust God? Then no God at all and if there is no God then there is no hope.

"Emily, you mustn't give way to despair." As if he has heard my thoughts. "Today we'll reach Nan-yang. There's hope there. There is always hope. God will provide. God *will* provide." I cannot look at him. William, you *are* guilty and still you are playing the faithful servant. "Emily, please don't cry. Think how far we have come in four days. It has not

153

been long." It has been an eternity. "Think of James."

See James through my tears, asleep on Martha's lap. She staring as if she sees nothing, hears nothing. But he's right. Don't cry. Don't give in. Be strong and stay alert. Look to save yourself. Save James. We shall not die.

"We reach Nan-yang today?"

"Yes, tonight. The magistrate there will put everything right again."

"Nan-yang!" It is the driver's taunting voice again as he recognizes the name of the city on our tongues. He has given us no peace today. "Not long now. You know what is waiting for you in Nan-yang, don't you?" He turns and bends and leers at us through the opening in the cover. He draws his finger across his throat and screams with laughter.

Yes, be strong. If we're going to be done to death by people such as these, at least don't make it easy. Fight back. And do not show your fear.

"Turn round, driver. Your job is with the mules. We'll report you as soon as we reach the city."

The man makes a vile gesture and William puts his hand on my arm to keep me from further remark. Why doesn't he *do* something?

"We'll pray for the man's soul and pray that God will give him grace enough to get us at least into Nan-yang."

Martha joins in William's prayer. And yet she still looks as if she sees nothing, hears nothing. Pray then for the poor beast if you want to. He has less chance of cleansing his black soul than we have of getting off this burning plain.

The other one, the sullen, silent one walking out there in the sun. He's frightened of Martha, too. She spoke to him again last night — I saw her. What could she have said to make him shake his head and back away? William saw her, too. That was when he brought her back inside the doorway where we had to sleep. *Was* it last night? When we were all so tired. And they came back in, those two, Martha and William — she like a blind dog following him — they came back in and started to pray for sinners everywhere. To pray. And James just gone to sleep and all of us needing sleep like

154

a drug that we craved and they praying. William said later she was trying to spread the word when she spoke to the guard. He looked askance when he said it. Almost embarrassed.

Yes, she is mad. She is.

Well, she hasn't scared these two away yet. They've got us this far. Or are they sticking with us just to see us executed? This one taunts us all the time with it. That we shall not get out of Nan-yang alive. He said an imperial edict is out to have us all destroyed. All foreigners. All Christians. Why should it be official? The people will do it anyway. Sometime. All this week the hostility towards us has been like fed flames, crackling higher and higher. Each time we stop, the people are ruder, more abusive. They have stolen from us again, taken our quilts, our shoes. We shall be stripped next time a crowd closes on us, I know it.

William has some money, a little, left hidden. But we can't buy much with it, and water's practically impossible. We have had nothing since yesterday noon, and that only *hsiao-mi chou,* the sludge from the bottom of the millet pot. The people of Honan are little better than the murderers in Shansi. Shansi. The driver said the governor was rounding up foreigners like hogs for the slaughter. He said it would happen everywhere, has started already. Not a foreigner left alive in Chihli, he said. It could be true. Oh, God, what is waiting for us in the city?

Without warning, Martha leans over to the driver. He stops the cart. James rouses and comes over to me while Martha climbs down. What is she doing? The driver is clucking the mules ahead.

"No —"

He turns round and leers at us again, pointing out to the side, making a filthy allegation about Martha and the other guard. I look through the slats of the cover and see them walking there in the road. The guard, the surly one, Hsi-lien, is walking briskly, keeping his eyes fixed on the way ahead. His expression is hard to make out but it is clear he does not want her near. Is it fear or plain annoyance? Or is it revulsion?

Martha with her long legs has no trouble keeping pace. Her

155

look is urgent, passionate, as she talks to him. Closer now, against the cart, as if he wants protection. She talks in his strange plains patois: "You must listen. The news I have is for you. Jesus loves you. Are you hungry? Pray to Jesus. Are you tired? Pray to Jesus."

"Come inside, Martha." I speak through the slats. She's mad, antagonizing him like that. Hsi-lien pushes her roughly away and she trips, but she's going right back to his side. William is frowning and looking nervous. For us, no doubt.

The cart stops suddenly. We're at a bridge and there is a food stall here.

"Miss Coleridge! Come inside. I order you!" William hisses now, afraid she will draw attention to us, but there is only an ancient food vendor out there and an idiot child lying on its side like a dog in the sun.

Martha steps round to the back of the cart. "She has rice over there. I'll buy some, Doctor, if we have enough."

"Let the guards do it. I'll give them the cash when they come back."

But the guards are already settling down in the shade of a canopy there and sucking at their bowls of rice. "I doubt whether they'll do anything for us now," Martha says. "I gather we've progressed from *foreign devils* to *first-class hairy devils*. Your fault for that beard that's appearing." William gives her a string of cash and she goes to buy the rice while we sit in the cart. Mad or not, she behaves most strangely. And what was that intimacy all about? If they have been guilty, would she give it all away with those few cosy words? And if William had the gall to seduce her, wouldn't he also have the gall not to blush like a schoolboy when she speaks to him?

Since no notice is being taken of us we get out and stand in the shade of the cart. We eat the rice that Martha brings and drink the bowls of boiled water. I think about the evil, the dysentery, that came on me before. The thought that the water, despite its name, *k'ai shui*, might not be boiled is almost enough in itself to quench my thirst.

We're not far from the approach to Nan-yang. We stand

156

with our bowls in our hands and stare out across the great plain that gasps its scent of burnt grass into the hot air against the sun. Useless grass burning itself out where the bright green millet stalks should stand. Endless heat, endless burning, endless waste. Endless despair. Nothing about Nan-yang feels good to me.

"Get up!"

Our escort is back. They've been talking with the food vendor and they're looking more sullen and hostile than ever. What did she tell them? They treat us like animals for market, shouting and shoving to get us back in the cart. The jolting and the creaking begin again. And we move so slowly, passing each rock, each blade of grass singly. Every one grass in the field.

Martha begins to sing again. Look at the way William watches her. As if she were a saint. If she sings like that when we reach this next place, she'll have us all stoned to death. James loves her singing. Oh James, to see you smile. He sings too, his hoarse voice following hers, not quite matching in time, a child's foot in the print of an adult's.

Oh, James. You don't know. Please God you may never know.

There are people out there on the road now. Voices shout as we go by. I think they know who is in the cart, what class of devil. That was what the food vendor was telling our men: an attack is planned. I am sure. That's why they look so nervous.

"No!" Hsi-lien sidling away, trying to lose himself in the crowd that is gathering.

"William, the guard! Look!"

William still looking through the slats of the shade. "We have a mightier protector than that poor devil."

No. Jump down.

"Emily!"

He mustn't get away. Push past them. People everywhere, pressing. He mustn't. He's our passport. There. Run. Past these. Catch his sleeve. Cling on. He turns. There, I thought

157

so: he will not lose face; he says he was going for water, going to bring us some.

Play my part. "Yes, yes. Water in cart. Water in cart."

He is coming back as I tug. Oh, he is coming back. Listen. Martha's voice rising above the babble. See how they leave a wide ring around the cart as it moves slowly forward. Oh, she is not mad. She is inspired. And look at my guard, the face of a boy caught scrumping. It's too absurd. I am laughing. Laughing. And look at the people parting like the Red Sea. I cannot see for my tears of laughter.

SPILL THE BLOOD OF THE FOREIGNER. THE TA TAO HUI SHALL BURN AND KILL. They are everywhere. Torn papers with their black characters, hanging from doorways, tacked to gates, stuck on barrows.

Our death warrants.

The crowd is vast now. We have not been alone since the guard tried to make off outside the city. The whole world is alerted to our existence and we try to hide like fleas under a mat. BY IMPERIAL COMMAND: it is official. Some of the posters bear a date: ON THE TENTH DAY OF THE SIXTH MOON. EXTERMINATE THE FOREIGNER.

We are vermin.

The tenth day of the sixth moon. Passed, then? No, of course not. We are in their sixth moon. Saturday was the fourth day —

"William, did you see the date on that poster?"

"Yes, that would be . . ."

Each of us makes a calculation. No one tells the answer: the day after tomorrow.

"Look." Martha is pointing and we see some figures pushing through the crowd. Dressed all in white calico, white cords about their waists, their feet bound in white. Mourners. A funeral. The people step back to let them through. No funeral but ours, our guard the cortege, our cart the hearse. The tumbrel. They take up places here on either side of our cart. They lift their heads, open wide their mouths and begin a long slow howl. We hold hands.

158

"In Thee, O Lord, do I put my trust . . . Bow down Thine ear to me . . . for Thou art my rock . . . Pull me out of the net . . ." William's voice is nothing against their wailing. What use can it be, praying, when God allows it even to begin?

But William doesn't stop; his voice a heartbeat, the wailing a ringing in the ears. I want to pray for James's sake but I cannot. My tongue is frozen between my teeth and my hands are bonded in William's in Martha's. I freeze with fear. But James doesn't need my prayers. He rests his face against William's chest, listens to the beat of the words, the reassuring hammer blows. He trusts. He trusts because he does not know. He is the little child I would become — except that I know and it's destroying me. Well, his trust shall not be broken. They shall not harm him. No, if it should come to that I shall do the deed myself and no guard, no William, no Martha shall stop me.

This is the yamen. The red walls are plastered with proclamations. The tenth day of the sixth moon. The tenth day.

But the guards are leaving us, going round to a door in the wall and leaving us here unprotected. The mourners still stand at the four corners of our cart. Ululations hoarse and ugly escape from their throats into the noise of the crowd. The people still leave a charmed circle around us — but they will not stand away forever.

The gate opens. The people begin to yell at the mandarin who comes out. The circle closes in. The mandarin makes his way to us, rips a notice from the side of the cart, reads it aloud:

" . . . *out of the province of Honan. Never to return.*"

The noise is overpowering. The people cannot have heard all of it. But he stills them. He raises his arms. The people are quiet.

"*Never to return.* This is quite plain. The devils are sent here to die."

A great shout goes up. The circle is upon us but the mourners send up an earth-heavy shriek. They are at the mules' halters. We are moving. Dear God, we are moving. We are inside the gates.

William's voice stops with the crash of the gates. What do

159

we pray for now, William?

Climbing down from the cart, we look all about us. Nanyang. Its heart. The yamen courtyard. The mandarin doesn't speak to us but strides off, his narrow coat flapping as he walks towards the offices. We smile wanly at each other, surprised to be still here. He leads us right through the building to a small room on the other side, an antechamber with a row of chairs to the right, facing the inner door.

William bows and says, "Thank you."

Speak before the man goes. "We wish to see the hsienling." Scorn. The mandarin turns on me with searing scorn.

"Thank you," says William again and the mandarin goes.

"Emily. You must put down your fears. Trust. Become as a little child . . ."

"But you're so resigned. You will let them obliterate us. We must act."

". . . as a little child," he repeats, "and allow our dear Father to know what is best for us."

The door opens and a tall figure bows very slowly, very low. The shaven head. Yes, it is. When he looks up, the face is like the face of a stranger in a dream, seen again in the morning. It is Chang-ch'ao. William and I bow — I hear his sharp intake of breath, Martha is kowtowing, her forehead touching the floor. Chang-ch'ao makes no protest but accepts the tribute.

Martha and I retire with James to one side of the room. I watch the two men opening their conversation, exchanging all the compliments of custom. Chang-ch'ao has a lot to answer for. William has not asked him how or why he is here. He doesn't even seem to be surprised that he is here. Chang-ch'ao is beautifully, ineffably kind and courteous.

"Your safe arrival has given me great pleasure. My servants were of some assistance through the city, I trust."

"The mourners were your men?"

"Indeed. I asked for a special guard to be posted for your protection but the sub-prefect here in his wisdom declined. Without offending the excellent Sung, I could think of no better way of keeping the curious at a distance."

160

"Your Eminence has met with the sub-prefect?"

"I have been here for two days now. I wanted the way to be ready for you, to smooth your passage. There is little, however, that I have been able to accomplish."

"Your Eminence has been petitioning the authorities on our behalf. I am grateful."

"As I said, Doctor, I have achieved little. Sung is not to be moved easily out of the deep ruts carved for him by the wheels of his office."

"Then I'm most grateful, I'm sure, for your efforts."

Why doesn't he ask him directly? *Are we to live?*

"Sung has consented to renew your passports and to alter slightly the wording which has caused you so much tribulation since you left Hsiang-ch'eng. He will not, however, issue the regular *yün-shu* but these I have here are very close."

Red borders, perhaps the same cards; they look identical. The subtle slip of words will not give pause to a mob along the road.

"Thank you," William says.

"I have also persuaded Sung to furnish you with an escort as far as Fan-ch'eng. Four men. He will personally provide the two runners to replace those who deserted you."

"Your Eminence, you have been more than kind to us."

"It is a small thing. Enough. We should go now to Sung."

They leave us. Martha looks not one whit moved, not in the least surprised by Chang-ch'ao's appearance here in Nan-yang.

"Mama, has Papa gone to the place of execution?" asks James with his devastating innocence.

"My darling, no. He's gone to meet a very important man."

"The Lord?"

Martha stifles a laugh. "Oh, James," she says, and her laughter is barely in check, "you are your father's son."

"No, James, an important man who's going to help us here on our journey."

James looks perplexed.

"But Emily, that's exactly what the poor child thought he meant. You wouldn't think it at all strange, would you, dear,

161

to see our Savior in a magistrate's cap speaking with your papa?"

Really, at times she is almost blasphemous.

"Here, climb on this chair, James, and you can watch the servants in the yard."

The boy is very good. He doesn't speak any more about Lin-sao — about Mercy. What empty places in his heart.

Martha would like to continue guying William through the child. But I won't let her: "Martha, you didn't seem surprised by Chang-ch'ao's appearance."

"Why, no, Emily. Didn't William tell you his plans?" *I won't answer that.* "Didn't you wonder why Chang-ch'ao didn't bring us our passports personally at Hsiang-ch'eng?" *Yes, I wondered.* "He had already started ahead of us. The other monk, the young one, told William when he sent us outside to sit in the little garden. Chang-ch'ao was being really rather mysterious about the whole thing but I think he didn't want to put undue emphasis on the importance of our getting through."

"It seems as if you and William have had your secrets, too."

"Emily, it was for your sake. William is the kindest man in the world. He was mad with worry when you were taken ill outside Hsiang-ch'eng. He thought he was going to lose you."

"But I'm not a child. Why do you both hide things from me? Our lives are in constant danger — may I at least have the privilege of knowing the circumstances of our deaths?"

"Oh, you are a great tragedienne. That's exactly why William wouldn't let me tell you. Chang-ch'ao was going on ahead to smooth our path, to prepare the magistrate in each place for our arrival, putting our case to him before the mobs could put theirs. It was all in our favor but William knew you'd just put the blackest construction on it. He said you would read it as proof of our imminent destruction and he wanted nothing to stand in the way of your complete recovery."

"And you are better, aren't you, Mama?" James heard only the last part of Martha's speech.

"There. James is always on my side."

And William too, it seems. What am I to make of it? She paints her lover as my loving husband. What to think?

"Emily?"

"I was just thinking. James is right. I am better now, yes. There's no need to keep anything from me. Anything at all. I am strong, Martha. Not like you but in my own way. I shan't give up easily."

"Oh, Emily," she grips my two hands in hers, "I know it, I know it. We shall all survive."

Perhaps. But that is not what I meant.

The same two guards. After food and a night's rest in a clean room, how optimistic we were — and how disappointed this morning by these men. I had — we all had — hoped to leave them behind in Nan-yang and have four new men. We have two, the usual ragged, underfed, underpaid scurf, but we still have the other two. Not of their own volition. They make that plain enough, scowling, snarling. Either they held out for a mighty payment or the magistrate used some other spur. If they are criminals they would have no choice but to do the magistrate's bidding. If they themselves are criminals . . .

The blackest construction. But I try to sight the danger, to fix it, in order to escape it. William goes blindly on, puts all his trust in prayer. Martha, I think, wouldn't even deign to pray if it weren't for William. Martha believes her life is her own. And she is looking to end it. She doesn't need to pray about it. But I neither have faith nor can I pray for it. Is that what William calls the blackest sin? Despair. Believing in oneself alone. But what else is there? Who can explain to me the news they brought this morning of the slaughter at Kao-t'ing fu? The Gordons, the Crofts, the Haddlingtons . . . Fifteen, twenty of them. The blood soaking away into the sand of the roadside, the eyes of the children watching, unable not to watch until the soldiers, out of breath, turn on them also.

Tell me now to be as a little child, William. Tell me not to mistrust — you who trust no one — these surly, dirty men who wish to be rid of us. Tell me not to remember how many times the hungry people have come sniffing about us like

163

starving dogs. Tell me not to remember Mercy under her pile of stones.

Tell me to forget tomorrow is the tenth day of the sixth moon.

Whatever Chang-ch'ao said, however kind he was, giving us food, money for the journey, whatever he wishes us to believe, he can't stop the Boxers, or make it rain, or change the order of the days. Chang-ch'ao said there would be no more trouble. He said one hundred and twenty li at the most from Nan-yang to Hsin-yeh, our last stop before the border. We could make it in a single day if we were lucky. He said. And, after that, two short days more of travel and those in the province of Hupeh where the benign influence of its beloved and smiling viceroy would draw us smoothly like lilies on a stream, he said, towards Fan-ch'eng. Fan-ch'eng and the boats that would carry us down the twisting Han to safety. The worst was over, Chang-ch'ao said.

Kind, yes, but Chang-ch'ao doesn't have to live his words, to make this journey with us. Didn't have to climb again into that bone-breaking cart, didn't have to set out again past the Boxer proclamations and see the eyes of the beggars outside the gates turn on him with hatred. These things are not for Chang-ch'ao. He'll never have to watch the mongrels at the bodies of abandoned children and know that the atrocity is laid at his feet by those who see their turn is next in the famine. But we see it and we know it. And what reason is there, on the eve of the day of execution, to hope for mercy from the people when they believe us guilty?

It is late in the day and we are so far unmolested, but wherever we stop we feel the vibrating buzz of hatred like the beating of a million wings in a vast cage of locusts. So many and such power, the thin bamboo ribs will never hold them back. The guards sense it, too. At first, the two new men — boys — made a show of drawing their long knives when we reached a village. Now they think better of associating themselves too closely with us and skulk a little distance away, hoping perhaps that the crowd will force a separation from us, the first step in what they have not the courage to

164

do for themselves. Yet we haven't been harmed, though the people here are starving, aching with hunger and still the rains have not come and still the sun beats on the hard earth. Perhaps the people are waiting for the most propitious day, the official day, to fling us at their gods and make it rain.

The town of Hsin-yeh isn't far. We can see the bridges now that span the shallow trough of the Pei, wide graceful spans supporting the shabby stalls and booths assembled there or built out, lodged like nests in the stonework. Something is left here of the Pei Ho, though it runs low in its bed, shamefaced and sneaking, before making its paltry offering to the Han further down. Little use this water must be to the acres of crusted lands that rise away like the backs of giant tortoises on either side.

I can see a crowd of people, bending as if they are working. But they can't be. There's nothing to harvest; the ground is shut like a clam in the sun against a further planting. They are working, cutting the dry reeds that fringe the bank. They have an idol out there, too, and that is a man's voice chanting.

"What are they doing?"

We are slowing down. William and Martha put their fingers to the slats and look out at the people on the bank.

"Look at the animals! Look at the dogs!" James is excited and pointing out of the front of the cart past the driver's shoulder. There is a pile of straw figures at the side of the road. The older people sit on the bank, tying the dry reeds into dogs the size of a child's doll.

"What's happening?"

"There must be a procession," says Martha. "Have you never seen the dogs before? They're offerings. They'll be carried in the rain procession."

We have stopped. Some of the people are turning round.

"Who's inside?" shouts a man.

"We should show ourselves." Martha speaks in a low voice.

"Travellers," replies one of the guards.

The guard, it is the youngest one, says quietly, "Foreigners." He does not say *devils* but the people catch the word from the air and leave their tasks.

165

"Yang kuei tze! Yang kuei tze!" We hear it repeated excitedly, urgently, all around us.

I hold James tight and I hiss at the driver: "Move on!"

The man who shouted starts to intone the Boxer slogan:

"Foreign blood
Must be spilled . . ."

William closes his eyes. I turn back from the driver, see Martha going to the opening at the back of the cart. No. She pulls the mat aside.

The noise stops. There is the charmed circle again, the people stepping back, staring, some looking at their feet, embarrassed. We are moving. Slowly. The people watch. Martha waves. She waves. She takes us to the very brink of disaster — and she has perfect balance.

Safely past. We sigh, breathe, praise, smile. But, of all of us, only James allows the good spirits to settle in comfort. William wipes the sweat from his face and, frowning, looks out through the gap to the road ahead, the dry flagged snake of road that is dragging us into the city. Martha settles back on the floor and the animal alertness in her eyes is blinked away and she stares again, vacantly, with a strange, drawn look, an intensity of expression as if she is concentrating on something deep inside, under her ribs. I feel the tightness of apprehension return to my neck, the dryness to my mouth.

A procession: the word brings no ill-defined unease this time but a particular danger clearly traced on the faces of the people; they see us as their props, the stock-in-trade of ritual, sent on purpose by the provident gods to aid in the performance, to be rendered, broken, back to them when it's over. No, the people won't miss the nice significance of our arrival here on the day of their procession, the eve of the official extirpation of the foreigner.

All day I have been wishing to see Hsin-yeh, to pass another stage in our journey; now I see the walls and I want only to make them recede, smoke away like bricks of incense, vanish. Let me wake up in another place.

166

It is hard to remember the sequence of events that brought us here; one remembers only the sequence of pain. We stopped, I remember that. And the guards ran off, just as they did before, to the yamen. But then it is confusion: James's skull rocking back against my teeth when the mob outside hurled its weight against the cart, the scratches when the cover caved in and the bamboo broke across our faces, then the scraping and the bruising as they dragged us from the cart. I remember a string of phlegm hitting my cheek. I remember hands from every direction, pulling, pushing. I remember James's squeals and my thought that it was my own fingernails cutting into the flesh of his arm as I tried to hold on to him. And then the blows, this time from the soldiers, Hsin-yeh men, who beat with sticks on our backs and drove us like criminals before them into the yamen.

It is not clear what will become of us. I do not understand what has happened to our own guard. We've not seen the magistrate and we've seen only a spokesman for the soldiers, a great, ugly lout, looking more like a Mongol than a Honanese and carrying his filthy opium pipe in here with its sickening stench fouling the room. He spoke a coarse language that only Martha could make sense of but we all understood when he demanded money. Look at us, in rags again. How did he know William still has Chang-ch'ao's money on him?

The man said the procession means special protection for us tonight, means extra payment to get us out of the city tomorrow. He demanded fifteen tael and William began to barter with him. No denial. No lies to save his family. He bartered. He might have as soon climbed in the drum tower and announced the exact sum he has tucked inside his cholera belt. Well, the man has gone now — to consult, he said. Oh William, so righteous, so right, so never wrong — what will become of us?

"Is your lip still hurting, James? Try not to touch it."

Try not to look forward. Help my rabbit now. Make the hours gentle for him in this room, this cell. Martha is staring at James with great empty eyes. She groans hoarsely and turns

167

her head away. The sweat is standing out on her forehead, on her bare arms. O God, our last hours and I have spent them on hatred.

"Martha. Are you all right?"

She looks up at me, surprised. "Yes. It's only the heat."

But she is shivering, shaking with her teeth jammed together again. It is a state of nervous shock, it must be. How can I help her?

"Is there something I can do for you?"

"For me? No, dear, nothing. There's nothing."

She gets up. She goes to the bowl of brown water that we all have sipped from and she puts her face in it, once, quickly, then she pats her face hard, many times, with the sleeve of the jacket that I put round her shoulders.

The soldier is coming back. I can hear him. Yes, it is him. "Nine taels," he says as soon as he is past the door. He says something else but Martha will not translate it.

William answers him in Mandarin — absurdly formal: "My friend, nine taels is many times more than we should begin to consider. Should you have a serious interest, however, in our safe arrival at Fan-ch'eng, we should be prepared to pay exceptionally well, make no mistake. The rate is five hundred cash per day per man. We need two men to the border. Only half a day at most."

"Likin barrier."

"We shall be asked to pay the tariff when we reach it, my friend. It is not your job to collect it."

"Procession dues."

"You are mistaken. Foreigners are exempt and you know it. Your suggestion verges on insult. Let us discontinue this conversation. It is time I saw the Hsien."

William repeats his wish and the man laughs.

"Magistrate will not see foreign devil. Magistrate is important man. He will not see you."

"Then you must tell him that my party will take the matter up with the viceroy at Hankow."

The man looks unmoved. William turns to Martha.

"Miss Coleridge, can you make the fellow understand?"

168

Martha explains in Honanese and the man's expression changes.

"Foreign devils not at Hankow. Foreign devils not out of Hsin-yeh." He slams the door angrily.

As she finishes whispering the man's last words, Martha's eyes are filled with huge tears. Martha crying? But she's not. There's no sound. She isn't even moving. Only great heavy tears roll, one after the other from her eyes.

Go to her. Put my arm round her burning shoulders. She rests her head in infinite desolation against me.

William turns from the door and sees us. His voice is tight, hard.

"This is no time to give way. We have to hold on." He begins the Lord's prayer. Martha's lips move soundlessly. And the tears still fall onto the grimed, brown skin of her knuckles. I don't care if she's been with him. We're all equally alone. We must hold each other.

We can hear the procession now. It could be Tsehchow again. Wave upon wave. Out there burning away the dark with their torches and flares, routing the devils with their gongs, licking the feet of their gods with their base, worthless dogs of straw.

William's praying stops. He goes to the window to look through the break in the lattice. But now his voice comes again, choked, stricken:

"Have mercy upon us, Oh Lord . . ."

I leave Martha. Go to him. There is nothing but a courtyard outside. Ah, no. Now I see it . . . hanging in the black sky . . . the moon. Look at the moon. It's red. I turn back towards Martha and James. "I know," she says. "A blood-red moon."

James is awake, yelping, excited, wanting to see it — the portent. It glows with a sickening, stomach-turning red. Blood burning. Oh God. What is it? What is it? It pulses with a dark crimson, a heart laid on black silk. For the empress.

"Come away," says William. He draws us from the window.

"What does it mean?"

"Nothing, Emily," answers Martha.

169

"It is a sign to prepare ourselves."

"Of course it isn't, Doctor."

Martha stands up. "It's not a sign. Do you think God will send us confidential messages? His own private telegraph?"

"Martha!"

"Well, really, Doctor Bancroft. You're as benighted as those poor people out there. Of course it isn't a sign. It's an atmospheric phenomenon. *They* think it's a sign, those poor ignorant souls. They'll read it as a sign and so much the worse for us. That's where the connection lies."

"Comes to the same thing, I'd say."

The door opens. William looks almost triumphant, would look triumphant had our own executioner walked in; but it's four men, the ugly one bringing another with him and our two original guards from Hsiang-ch'eng.

"Ah, Tsen Tao," William says to our driver, "you can explain to this officer. Our contract is already settled to Fan-ch'eng, is it not?"

Tsen is going to a table in the corner, unwrapping a bundle. He shrugs. "Can tell nothing. In Hsin-yeh now. Hsin-yeh men tell what to do." He will not look at us. Neither of our men will. They busy themselves at the table and will not meet our eyes.

"Look, our contract must be worth at least four thousand cash to you. It's a long way back to Hsiang-ch'eng and many days to wait for reimbursement. I'm prepared to give you two thousand cash at Fan-ch'eng, five hundred of which shall be earnest money, paid tonight, if you'll settle with these men and leave with us at first light."

"No more barter." The Hsin-yeh man steps forward. "Not come to barter. Offer closed. Come to watch until hour of execution."

That is not true. It can't be. We've not seen a single official.

"I don't understand."

"Yes, understand. If no rain, die. Die in morning."

"That can't be true," Martha says to us. "The magistrate would have made more of it. He's much more likely to be holding on to us in case things get too sticky for him. A little clutch of foreigners might prove more than useful if the rains don't come soon."

But she misses the point. The magistrate is not involved. "I don't think it has anything to do with the magistrate; we're in some kind of servants' quarters. I doubt whether he even knows we're here. They probably told him a pack of lies about the fighting at the gates."

"Either that," says William, "or he's given us over entirely to these scum. Like Pilate, washed his hands of us."

"Close mouths. No speaking," says the Hsin-yeh man and he joins the others at the table. They turn their backs on us. Pretend we are not here. What are they up to? They roll out their mats on the floor.

"William, we can't be their responsibility. We must get to the magistrate. We —"

Teeth in my lip. He has struck me, the Hsin-yeh man, wheeled round and hit me with the back of his hand outstretched. My mouth. William whitefaced. Rage? But the man doesn't even look to see how he hurt me. He bends again over the table. We are curs, vermin. William says nothing. But what are they doing? One of them setting up a lamp. An opium lamp. Here in this room. Whisper now.

"William, don't let them."

"Shhh," Martha's voice, low. "Rather that than see them building a pyre. Leave them alone."

The short one is pulling his ragged tunic over his head. The others too. They are undressing.

"Gentlemen!" William's voice is as uncertain as I have ever heard it. Martha and I turn away while he continues, faltering. "I must beg you to remove yourselves unless you make yourselves decent."

There is no response. I turn and catch sight of their bodies, slick and greasy, reclining in the dull glow of the lamp.

The fumes begin to invade the room. "Pray to God," William says to us, "this cannot last."

"Yes, it can," Martha answers. "And we may as well rest. They're not going to trouble us any more now." She goes, without concern, to settle down in the far corner of the room,

171

her back to the smokers.

"Martha is right." I comb James's hair with the little wooden comb and try to keep him from looking at the men. I make him lie down with his head on my lap. William joins us.

The smell of the opium is everywhere. Fetid and sweet. Using up the air in our stifling room. Nothing to breathe but the nauseous fumes. Take small, shallow breaths, hardly dare to fill my lungs. But James's back rising and falling as he takes the greedy draughts of sleep. The smoke makes the room seem hotter. Even the voices of the men seem to add to the thick heat. They are arguing. I feel trickles of sweat running down under my braid, sliding between my breasts, making my cut lip burn and the backs of my legs itch with salt.

"Miss Coleridge," William motioning Martha to come back again. She is up. Pacing back and forth close to the men. She takes no notice. Paces slowly, surely on her broad, bare feet, softly, looking neither right nor left.

"I think she's trying to listen to them. Leave her."

The men are leaning closer to each other. Their voices lower now. They are in agreement. All telling each other it is good, it is very good. They are conspiring against us. Martha will tell us.

"*T'ang-hsia!*" one of them shouts. Jumps up. Martha looks away from his nudity and comes back again.

"Go to sleep," he shouts. "All all. Go to sleep." He goes to the window and pushes a pair of ragged trousers into the crack in the lattice. Protest? It does not seem to matter.

Martha's voice coming from far away. "Do as he says, only stay awake!"

With James on my lap, I try to slide down and rest my head on my elbow. Wait for Martha to tell us. How easy to wait, float, on a long line, a buoy at sea. So easy now. Nothing to want, except sleep and that comes on its own steep tide, rising, covering my eyes . . .

". . . to kill us." Martha's voice. Stay awake.

"What?" I can't hear my voice. Did I speak or dream that I said the word?

"Emily! Were you sleeping? That's the last thing to do, just

172

what they want."

"I'm sorry — it's the fumes. Please go on." Each word I speak tugs on the long line that is floating under the dark surface.

"You're falling right into their trap. They're planning to kill us. The magistrate is occupied with the procession but he knows we're here so they won't dare to rob us or kill us outright for fear of being discovered. They'll lose the rest of the official payment if anything happens to us."

Means nothing. *Let me sleep.*

"Emily! Please, whatever happens you must stay awake."

"Then," William's voice asking the question I cannot put together, "then what *are* they planning?"

"They're going to burn as much opium as they can and then when we fall asleep they plan to smother us. No traces, no repercussions. They can have our money, be rid of their irksome duty and collect not only their full payment but a little extra to keep them quiet when they begin to say we died of suffocation in the wretched conditions here."

"But we could —" It is hard to speak, "— we could *give* them money."

"No, it wouldn't work. We can't be sure of getting more and once they have our silver we're trapped: they'll have no reason left to take us on."

Martha seems to know. I trust her. William nods.

"I think you're right, Miss Coleridge. But I think we're already in the trap and we have been given the grace of at least a warning to prepare ourselves."

"No." Martha and I speak together.

"No, the execution is a threat, a lie," she says. "You forget that the magistrate has been busy with the procession. If we can just get through until morning, we may be safe."

Two of them getting up. Coming over. They have remembered we're supposed to be sleeping. They pull on their clothes as they curse us.

"Close mouths. Snakes." One of them gesturing with a club. "Prisoners sleep now. Die in morning. Die now if not sleep." He clutches Martha's hair at the base of her neck and

173

spins her round away from us, facing the two remaining guards lying naked on either side of the lamp.

"Now close eyes," he says. And he and the other one, it is Hsi-lien, go out.

Yes, Martha's right. If we can just stay awake. Silence now except for the sputtering lamp. Nothing to disturb it. No wrenching, no tugging. Now my mind looks in, feels the heaviness, the ache of sleep. Nausea rising. From my navel up. Nausea sitting in an oval jellied bag under my ribs. In a smaller one in the hollow of my collar bone. Close my eyes. Hold on.

"Look after James, Emily. Listen to his breathing." Heavy, heavy. James heavy. His breathing heavy. Martha leaning across, fanning his face with a piece of broken mat, "Do it, Emily. You do it. Stay awake." My hand holding the mat. Too heavy.

Martha crawling across my legs to William, "Doctor Bancroft!"

The light blocked. The lamp smashed. Smoke everywhere. Another light in the doorway. Martha trying to wake William before it is too late. A body falling on Martha's back. Her voice choking out of her, strangled. They are killing Martha. They are killing her. All awake now. William breaking out of sleep. Tearing the fingers from Martha's throat. Reach for her arm. No — another guard. Behind William. Martha falling way. William still with his hands on her attacker.

"Look out!"

But he stops. Staring stupidly ahead. Blank. As if deciding what to do next, where to turn.

A scream. Whose? An unearthly shriek. And Tsen Tao pointing to William and William still staring, staring and suddenly looking down and bending his head towards a spot on the floor, bending, slowly bending, his hands not coming out to break his fall. Save him.

He falls on me heavily and he is wet. The men gabbling, babbling to each other, stumble over each other in their hurry to get out of the door.

William's face buried in my lap. James behind me pressing

close and roaring with uncontrolled terror. Martha tries to pull him away.

"Ah, William, William." I turn his face up. Still staring. Nothing there. Nothing staring at nothing. He is dead. "Ah, William."

"God help us now." No more shamming: Martha's prayer is real.

"Have they all gone?"

Martha looks outside. "Yes. They were afraid. The foreign blood . . ." She picks up the knife they used and wipes it carefully on the hem of her jacket.

How long now since either of us spoke? Everything is quiet. No sound in the yamen, no sound in the city outside, the procession long over and everyone sleeping.

"What do you think, Emily? It will soon be light. We should make it soon if we're going to do it."

I have made my decision. No one to tell me what is right, or moral, or godly. Oh, but William, now I want to uncover your dead face and ask you if it is all right, if you mind.

"Emily?"

"Yes. You're right, it may be our last chance. We should try."

"Thank you." Her voice is low. Is it hard for her, too?

Don't be offended, William. Look in our hearts. See why we do it. For life. That cannot be wrong.

Martha picks up James and he doesn't rouse, his mind deadened by the opium or deadening itself against the sight of William. I follow her outside, the door flung back on its hinges, the padding of bare feet, running, still reverberating in my mind. James hasn't woken. We stretch him out between us on the ground and we kneel. We are in the centre of a courtyard. Chambers in front of us and to our right might belong to the magistrate. They have to. He has to see.

Martha begins keening softly. I wait. And she begins to chant. Words we have heard against us on every side. Words of the Ta Tao Huei, the I Ho Ch'uan. Sinful words to false gods and I doing as she says, repeating after her the sacrilegious

175

litany.

> "Foreign blood must be spilled
> before the rain.
> We have spilled the foreign blood."
> *"We have spilled the foreign blood."*
> "Foreign devils against their own . . ."
> *"We have spilled . . ."*
> "Have turned and freed the blood . . ."
> *"The foreign blood . . ."*
> "Freed the rain . . ."
> *"We have spilled . . ."*
> "Rain shall follow blood . . ."
> *"The foreign blood . . ."*

Again and again and again. Repeating the blasphemy the injury to our God. And the sky *is* dark and dawn *is not* breaking as it should and Martha is right. It is going to rain. The blood-red moon brings rain, she said. It happened before. It could happen again. Today, the tenth day of the sixth moon, it *is* going to happen again.

There is a face behind the lattice up there. Someone is watching, listening. And above that face great leaden clouds are rolling up over the dragons of the roof trees, massing silently.

Chanting louder and louder. More faces behind the windows. Footsteps behind us, in the passage that leads to our room.

Don't be distracted. The rain *shall* come. Keep on, keep on. Yes, the footsteps running now, back from the room. Keep chanting. They've found William, found the blood. What will they do now? Kill us for the blasphemy against their gods while we blaspheme our own?

James turning over, stretching. Don't wake now. Don't.

> *"Foreign blood . . ."*
> "Rain for the seed . . ."
> *"We have spilled . . ."*

176

Yes it is. It is raining. Martha raising her hands. I raise mine.

"Foreign blood has brought the rain."
"We have spilled the foreign blood."

And now she is crying. Real tears. Rain spiking our hands, our faces. Everything blurred. Are the faces still there? Gone? The rain waking James. He climbs onto me. Like fear.

Ah, but look — Martha's hand reaches out and grips mine — there through the door in the opposite wall, we see two mules being made ready, standing in the quickly falling rain. They are for us. I know it. A servant running with a bundle, tying it to one of the saddles. Another boy, taking the halters, leading the animals this way. He calls out.

"Be quick! Get out of here!"

Oh, no need to worry — we shall be quick, my friend. James in front of me clutches instinctively at the mule's neck. The saddle sits badly but no time to change it. The servant is pointing to the gate through the other courtyard that will lead us out of here. No one else about. But faces at every window, watching through the rain. I feel them. Let it not be a trick.

"*Tsou pa!*" He really is afraid. The gate has been opened for us. We pass through.

"Stop!" The word freezes the breath in our bodies. Turn round. A boy running after us. He carries two straw capes. He thrusts them at us and says, "South," pointing down the narrow street. The capes are hooded. We put them over our heads and thank him, but he is already running back over the slippery flags.

"*P'ing-an*" — peace — calls Martha, and the boy turns once.

"Hold on, James." I kick the mule hard. It balks, tries to turn, finds its pace.

Martha sees my eagerness. "Don't let her run yet."

People about now, preparing, thank God, to go to the fields, every one of them hurrying, head down beneath the rain that falls in long pencils, heavily now. No one can see who we are unless, like nuns, we look at them full in the face.

The city gate is open for the people making their way out to the planting.

Now. Break into a run. Running now. Free. The mules run lumpily side by side and James shouts with excitement. Make him be quiet.

"Can you see if we are being followed?"

Martha turns, pushing back her hood, "Yes, several of them. On ponies."

No. It cannot be a trick. Too cruel. To be murdered out here in the life-giving rain?

"Hold tight, James. Don't move." I manage to turn and see at least six riders, hooded like us and keeping at an even distance.

"Slow down and face it out or run?"

"What do you think?" says Martha and she is smiling, exhilarated by the rain, the space, the morning we did not expect.

But we kick and kick and the mules won't run any faster. They are hot now, dashes of foam streaking their necks and a sharp, rich smell rising from them, mixing with the earthy scent of the soaked straw of our capes. We ride with our heads down, watch the softening earth splash away under their hooves. We have passed people, workers, already out in the fields, bending to the earth. Where did they come from, springing like shoots from the watered soil? From the city or not, it doesn't matter; we were nothing to them, shadows crossing the low sun, crows winging by; they had no time for remark.

Much slower now. The ground softening fast. The mules lazy, as if they feel they have given enough service, strayed far enough from the city.

Look back. But the men are no closer. Then they don't intend to overtake us. Another escort?

"They're for our protection," says Martha.

I nod. "Or for the city's protection — they're seeing us off." At least they won't come near.

Still raining. Thank God for the rain — if it is possible to thank God after what we have done. Is there a God to pray to still? Will He allow us to betray Him the way we did and still call on Him for shelter? Our duty is tied to our faith. Can we let go one, even for a moment, and not lose the other? Can we deny God and then a second time recant, turn our backs and turn again to find Him still there? The Lord heard the unspeakable profanities, the cries we uttered to the false gods, the graven images. Did He, like the watchers at the windows above the courtyard, listen to those profanities and believe them? Did He listen and did He send the rain in perverse and mighty testimony of His power — the unanswerable antiphon? What happened?

No one in the yamen doubted what happened, that we, Christian women, had killed one of our own, a friend, a husband, had made of him a sacrifice so fitting that the gods, placated, sent the rain. The servants and the lesser men believed it or we wouldn't be here. But the magistrate? An educated man? He was dissembling, he must have been, feigning belief so that he could snatch the perfect opportunity to get rid of us. Or perhaps not. What was there to stick in his throat, to stop him from swallowing our unholy concoction at a gulp? His pagan gods acceding graciously to our naive petitions for rain — are they more strange, less credible, than my angry, eavesdropping God piqued at the aspersions cast on His power and sending the rain to spite us?

I look back along the strip of road that shines like a lick of slip on the pottery floor. The figures of the riders are approaching fast.

"I thought they would turn back here."

"So did I."

We'll be at the Han in a little while, hire there the boat that will float us on to safety. If we can. Our soldier may not be so accommodating. Says he's not going to stay to help in that. But he's been good to us, poor boy. His luck wasn't with him back at the border when the six of them overtook us. We were right: they'd been officially detailed to see us out of the province and none of them relished the duty. They stood a little way off at the likin barrier, trying, without involving themselves too closely with us, to look purposeful and authoritative. It wasn't until Martha opened the bundle, found the silver, that their interest in us quickened. We begged them for more help on to Fan-ch'eng and, though none of them wanted to come, all of them were hungry. They couldn't, they said, legally escort us in Hupeh but they could tell off one of the party, one only, to go with us, the rest of them being content to settle for half pay. Well, the poor boy — he was the unlucky one, of course. The others wanted to take their share there and then but we refused, saying the boy would be paid for all. The toll collector took our part, someone else with an eye to a share.

I hope none of them gives the boy trouble when he gets back. He's been truly good, carrying out his duty without a murmur though I'm sure he curses it in his heart. He never speaks to us, won't even tell us his name, but he hired a covered cart for us, worked hard at the bargaining, closed a favorable deal and looked after our interests. Ever since then he has kept out of our way riding off to the left and coming in only when he sees the driver start to speak to us. Then he makes him turn his gaze back, get on with his job. He is, I think, desperately afraid of trouble.

We've made good time. Two days of good travelling from the border to here. We've avoided the inns and taken our meals along the way, eating only the small rations from the bundle while the men have found for themselves, though we do offer to share what we have. They've squatted to eat in the dusty shade beside the cart and we have stayed inside always, listening to the grumblings of the driver, who longs for the company he'd find at an inn, hearing gratefully the curt responses of the boy, who bravely tells the older man to mind his tongue and obey those who are paying him. Two days of travel, farther and farther from Honan, for which I thank God, from William. For which I weep. And do you mind, William? Is our escape working like salt in your wound, your death wound?

William.

We dragged your corpse into our profane charade. We forced you, dead, to collude in something you never, living, would have countenanced. Duplicity: the meanest of sins, prompted by cowardice, the meanest of instincts. And both, the sin and the weakness both, I thought for so long, for so long were yours. But Martha has told me. Here in the darkness of the covered cart, she has whispered her story, your story, how you tried to help her, always to help her, when she slipped by wretched accident from one addiction to another still more vile, how you never abandoned her even in her most base degradation — and how you tried always to shield me from what had become of my friend. And all the time I thought . . .

Oh William, forgive me. Oh God, forgive me for my thoughts. All mistaken. And I so cold to you, William. So cold. Believing you yearned for Martha, believing you deceived me. William. The thoughts I had of you before Hsin-yeh, before the blood-red moon . . . *Coward* I called you and — you know it now, I can't hide it — hated you. I am the coward. Lying, blaspheming, degrading your death to save my skin.

And Martha, what will become of her? No shame in our escape for Martha even though the plan was hers; her motives like pure water wash away the guilt: to free herself, she said, leaning across in the gloom of the closed cart, holding my hands in hers, that idiot ecstasy again on her face, to free herself in order to return, continue. I'd never have believed it except that I know she hasn't any choice. Not *wants* to return; has to. No room at home for her and her secret to hide. She'll be driven away, back here — to her salvation, her cast-iron salvation.

No saving grace for me, the false witness, lying even to myself, saying it was for James. It was for me I was saving my skin. Oh God, forgive me. William, you know everything now. Can you bear it forever, to hear the chant that denied your martyrdom, that gave the pagan to believe his was, indeed, the power and the glory?

What are they doing to you now? Let them leave your body

alone; it is broken, like the promises. And I, the most faithless servant, I am still alive.

Ah, William. Why you? Why not have let Martha die? As low as the meanest opium sot — why didn't you tell me? Why allow her the glory of confession? Now she's playing the sinner saved, the favorite of the Lord, carving out for herself the greediest chunk of heaven. And you, William, grasping and clutching at the outer edge, your only handhold a faith I have seen shaken almost from its roots, the most precarious hold there is on the affections of your God.

Ah, William. Why did you die?

I pull aside the cover at the front of the cart, look out through my tears past the driver's shoulders. The flat plain breaking away down to the trough the rivers make where they meet. And all the way down the stepped, shelving land to the river, the houses.

"I think this is Fan-ch'eng."

Martha looks. "It must be."

Fan-ch'eng. The last barrier between us and the freedom of water. The ground has not been softened here, is everywhere as hard as stone. Less rain than at Hsin-yeh but the people here are different. I don't feel the same menace in the air. Fan-ch'eng may prove me wrong. The towns are always difficult.

Descending now to the river, the cart taking the broad, broken, paved road that scythes the hillside in one great curve, almost surrounding the town. The river is crowded with boats — sampans, houseboats, some freight junks, little ferries — and yet there is scarcely any life. No produce to move. No one with money to buy it even were there any. No grain to sell or to buy. Everyone waiting for the skies to fulfill their promise. No money to spare, no goods to move, no reason to work. People look at us but no one bothers with us. Everyone waiting. Boats everywhere. The price should be reasonable.

James squeezes his face under my arm that holds back the cover. "Shanghai! Look at the boats!"

"No. Not Shanghai. Not even Hankow, my love. But we'll get there yet."

"Papa! Look at —"

Oh God. He forgets. Now see his face. Confusion. Death is an embarrassment. Like life.

"Papa has gone to look after Mercy for us. Do you remember? Look, I expect they're watching too. See all the sails on the other side. That is Siang-yang. It looks like patchwork."

The driver pulls up at a wharf where the boatmen squat and smoke and cook. They have almost set up their own township here, must not have moved in weeks. The soldier helps us down and Martha walks round to pay off the driver. He grunts and drives away, ignoring our goodbyes and thank yous.

We pay the soldier as discreetly as we can from our obvious — our inviting — silver. He is taking payment for the others, too, those who did nothing. He smiles for the first time. Takes James's hand.

"Lai-lai!"

"No! What are you doing?"

"It's all right," says Martha, her hand on my arm, restraining me, tactfully.

The soldier walks with James towards a corner of the wharf where some market stalls stand deserted. The food stalls. A woman sits on the ground and spread before her are some useless paper replicas, houses, furniture, carts, animals, even food. James points to a little paper cart and the soldier buys it, smiling. Smiling all his two days'-worth he has been too afraid to show. James comes running back and the soldier waves. *"P'ing-an,"* we say, and watch him walk away.

There are many boatmen. I wish the soldier had stayed to help us choose. They're looking at us with that rude objectivity, that indifference that stands on the very edge of hostility.

But the driver is coming back. Hurrying along on foot. He accosts Martha.

"This is not full payment."

"Oh, yes . . ."

"Not full payment. This is half payment."

"It is what we agreed."

"This is fare to Fan-ch'eng. Now you pay me back to

border."

"That is not the agreement and you know it."

"You pay full payment now. No good for you to keep money. I make sure no boatman take you."

"Keep your voice down."

"Give me full payment now or whole river hear me." He starts to stride up and down. Everyone is looking.

"Here."

"Martha, no!" She is giving it to him. "No. It's all we have."

The man snatches the money and grunts derisively. "All," he says.

"There. Now that *is* all." Martha hands him the little she had kept back. He spits, turns abruptly and goes.

"What now?"

"Get out of the public view, I should think," Martha says.

We make our way over to the empty stalls. Well, *what* now? That was the deposit on our passage to Hankow. We sit in the shade and stare out at the wharf and the desultory action there that already continues as if we had never appeared.

"I'm sorry," says Martha. "There was nothing else I could do. And I don't know what we're to do now."

"We have the promissory notes in the bundle still. The magistrate's word should be good enough to get us a passage."

"Not without a deposit. These men may be eager for work but they won't set out on nothing. And we have nothing. Not a single cash."

"Nothing to sell. I don't see what we can do."

"Well, I'm leaving it up to God. It's time we had some help."

I laugh at her despite the bleakness.

James is over at the old woman's paper goods again. He is trying to get back the cash for the cart. She is shaking her head. Poor thing. Probably hungrier than we are. She hands him a paper donkey to go with it. He comes back, unsure of whether this is good or not.

"Mama, she's saying something about Nan-yang. Come and listen."

I go over and kneel in front of her. Her eyes are rheumy,

cloudy. She tilts her head on one side. I am not sure if she can see.

"*Chi-le ma*, honored mother?"

She stares. I don't know what dialect she speaks. Repeat all the polite phrases I know. "*Ni-men hao?*" She is still staring. Perhaps she will recognize the name of the city. "Nan-yang. We come from Nan-yang. Nan-yang, Hsin-yeh, Fan-ch'eng."

Martha comes over to help. She bows, says, "Honored mother."

Now the old woman shows some recognition and begins to speak. She is making a gesture to indicate a child. I call to James and he comes. What is she saying, nodding so violently? "*Liangke waikuo nujen ho yike nan haitzu.*" — Two foreign women and a boy. She repeats it once, twice and stops. She is looking straight at me with bleary, marbled eyes. "Stay here," she says. "There is a monk looking for you."

We try to ask her more but she's busy congratulating herself on finding us and is saying again and again, "Yes, yes. Two foreign women and a boy."

We can get her to say nothing else and we go back to our shady spot.

"Do you think it's Chang-ch'ao she means?" says Martha.

"I don't see how."

"Neither do I. Even if he'd decided to see us through again from back at Nan-yang he couldn't possibly have made better time than us."

I scrape the dust at my feet with a little stick and have no answer. There's something even stranger to puzzle over.

"He would have to ride," she says, "day and night. Our stops have been hardly anything."

She would like me to answer, to help her to solve it. But she has missed it, this other thing. I prod at the dust to the rhythm of the words. *Liangke waikuo nujen . . . nan haitzu.* Two foreign women and a boy. How did he know? How could he possibly have known how many we should be? He didn't get to Hsin-yeh before us, and if he followed us there and found . . . and found what he did afterwards then there's no possible way he could have got that message — two foreign

185

women and a boy — down here to the dockside ahead of us. The words are like stones battering on William's body.

How did he know? How? It is as if William's death in Hsin-yeh was predestined, a universally acknowledged fact. I cannot cling to him any more. He was with me until the words. Absent merely. Not murdered, that was only a nightmare. I could forget. He was simply not here for the moment. But he was with me. He existed. Not any more. The words killed him. Raining down on him, covering him from sight. He no longer exists for me. I am without him forever. All that is on earth of him, a corpse with a torn hole in its side. A corpse in the hands of its murderers. Mutilated? Mocked? Dear God in heaven, protect his poor remains from violation. He only tried to serve. *I will pray.* Grant his body the reverence that is fitting as Thou hast granted his soul, I trust, *I do trust*, his last reward in heaven. Amen.

Stare out through the shimmering air to the sluggish river and the idle boats. A haze rising. The masts in air mirroring the movement of their own reflections. Everything barely, only just perceptibly, moving. Like the shadows on the bedroom wall. Tsehchow. Before it all began. All of them together now. Father and children. Don't let William be denied. Please God, all of them together.

But again the thought comes, like a rat in the night: why not Martha? Look at her. She is squatting on her haunches and she wipes the sweat from her face with the flat of her hand. She uses the same pose, the same gesture as the men outside crouching on the dock. Smoking. They smoke the seed of Satan and their laughter bubbles like foul water into the odorous air of the river. Not much more than animals. Martha no better. Though she speaks of it as a simple fact, in the past now, like a bad tooth pulled. But can one be whole after that — the reeking rot of it in the bone to stay, surely?

And yet Martha will be saved; that is not in question, never was. By her conduct she has excluded herself forever from the parsonage, the committee room, the church porch, but her self-inflicted exile is a double-sided document and written there on the other side for God alone to see is her promise to return and that, *that* is her ticket to salvation. Crazy Sister, saint and sinner, *l'idiote savante*, they were astute who named you.

Someone is coming. Martha gets up stiffly to speak to him. A boatman. They have difficulty understanding each other, make vague, half-hearted gestures that they know are no help to the words. James speaks to him. Martha and I do not recognize any of James's speech. We shrug. But the man understands. He smiles and speaks again. James is pleased. Martha whispers that she thinks they are speaking a language of the gutter. She is smiling.

James is trying to translate the man's words for us. It seems there is a boat and it is paid for.

"Let's not ask any more questions," says Martha.

We wave to the market woman, whether she sees us or not, and we follow the boatman. I ask James not to speak to him any more — surely he can't have understood the man. The boat leans against a tilting jetty. As we approach, a shaven head appears in the central well and the figure of a monk emerges. It isn't Chang-ch'ao.

He bows and greets us. His name is Sun Si-fa.

"All is in order." He has been inspecting our living quarters. Now he completes the contract with the boatman: the captain and his two men to transport us, two women and a boy, to Hankow in not more than twenty-eight days, a bonus to be paid, with interest, if they can return with a statement, signed by us and witnessed in Hankow, that the journey was completed in less time, an additional bonus if we are safely delivered by the seventh day of the seventh moon.

We wait patiently. The terms are nothing to us. It is important only to start. The deal is completed. We bow our thanks.

"Your Eminence, please have patience with my ignorance. You are sent by the revered Chang-ch'ao, are you not?"

"Yes, indeed. I am on my way across to Shen-nung-chia."

"Chang-ch'ao is indeed kind and gracious to show such close concern for us on our journey."

"He was anxious to ensure your safe passage from here since

187

he knew you would be travelling on without the doctor."

He knew? I don't understand. How to ask him in this polite Mandarin, *You know my husband is stabbed to death?* "He knew?"

"I believe so. His instructions were for me to arrange passage for two women and a boy."

"I see."

"Chang-ch'ao was very anxious to help. He wanted to do more at Nan-yang but he feared to give the doctor any great burden of silver that might be mislaid along the way, you understand. Since I happened to be coming directly . . ."

"Of course. He is — you both are — most kind. Please convey one hundred thousand thanks to him."

"It's nothing. I'm sorry I missed the doctor, your husband." He bows and wishes us a pleasant journey. The jetty sways slightly as he walks away. He stops and turns. "The captain will not start till morning," he says. "You will have to sleep on board tonight. These people are very superstitious."

Breathing. Like sighing of surf on shingle. Lapping. Water under the boat's bow. Creaking. Boards complaining under bare feet. Voices. Orders.

Open my eyes. The cabin rayed with thin bars of gray light that slip through the bamboo walls. James is next to me, his shoulders rising, falling, his breathing in soft love with the water. Dark form of Martha, lying flat, face down in her bunk, a thick lock of hair snaking over the edge. Slip my arm out from under James. Put on the same lice-infested jacket and trousers. Leave them sleeping.

The warped door scrapes open. Head of a sea-monster glowering down. Huge carved head, red eyes, dragon's mouth bared in a square snarl, curled tongue through fangs, the ornate stern of a huge junk looms over our houseboat. Moored here in the night to stare at us unconscious in our beds.

Bony shins and bare feet sticking out from shorn-off breeches, the men are padding over our deck. We lie in shadow still. The sunrise only just fleshing the air. Across the river the light falls on the mass of sails and spars. Behind them, the bare, stripped hills are made beautiful by the pink light. Every indentation, every cleft and fissure in the land colored one of a thousand shades from the purple of the black rose to the pink of a cat's lip.

A sudden commotion at the bow. Squawking, metallic cry of a cockerel. The men bending to it. Laughing. I stand close to see. Flash of a blade in the first shard of sun to strike through the boats. Two men stretch the cockerel by head and legs across the prow. The chopper comes down past the clattering wings and a jet of blood arcs out over the water. The captain tosses the head to follow while the cockerel's rusty squawk still echoes between the wooden hulls.

The men are grinning broadly. They smear the bow and the foremast with blood and tear out feathers to stick on it. They offer me some. "Good fortune, good fortune."

"No, thank you."

The captain now unstopping a jar. Wine. They pass a cup then cast the remains into the river, pleased with their sacrifice.

Blood and wine mingling in the water. The water mingling in the dawn light that breaks upon it. Dances. The voyage will be a good one. *I believe it.*

Epilogue

My Dear Emily,

*The willows outside my window are all alive today.
There is a blackbird singing there and a breeze is jangling
the chimes on the veranda. The rains have been good to
the earth and one goes about in a kind of suppressed ecstasy
as if one might burst into song at any moment. You'd
love it, Emily. I know what you said a year ago and I
understand, but if you were to leave Auldbury and come
here you wouldn't be able to help yourself. Your beloved
William, Edward and sweet, sweet Mercy would be with
you everywhere.*

*Since starting this my pen has been lying idle on my
desk for three days because what I have to say is hard.
There are things which perhaps will come as a shock to
you and things which you may not understand. I do not
pretend to.*

*I am at Hsiang-ch'eng, as you see. I did return to Jun-
ch'eng but I couldn't stay. The memories of that place
bore down on me like the weight of the mountain in a
slide of grief and it was all set off by a new horror. I
learned that my dear Mr. Tang had taken his own life.
How could I stay?*

*Emily, I can't describe to you my condition then. I
don't think in all our trials that I ever approached the
despair I felt then, alone in Jun-ch'eng. I shan't try to
explain my actions to you or the thoughts that led to them
but I ask you to believe only that I was driven by love.
Whether you believe it or not will not really matter; I
have slipped out of reach of either censure or approval, so
whatever you think, my dear, don't worry — and I say
this without bitterness — it can't touch me.*

*Well now, you wonder, knowing what a sinner I am,
what wickedness you're going to hear about now. Well,*

190

really nothing serious — nothing, anyway, that could harm another soul: I came to Hsiang-ch'eng and here I stayed. Just that. Chang-ch'ao was good. He took me in, of course. All the monks are good. The two or three old women, Buddhist nuns of course, who come and go here have healed me. I shall never evangelize again; the Christian church is safe from me — but Christ isn't. I talk to him often. (I haven't discussed that with the nuns yet but I don't think they'll turn me out.) I'm happy here. I shan't ever leave.

But none of this touches you so nearly as what I have to say next. Chang-ch'ao, who's been away for several months, came three days ago to tell me things he had kept hidden when he took me in. He said that the time for telling had not then arrived.

He told me first how he came on after us when he heard that a procession was in progress in Hsin-yeh, how he arrived on the morning, that dreadful morning, of the tenth day of the sixth moon. He told me how he found all his forebodings horribly fulfilled, the yamen in an uproar with officials fighting like cats and dogs over what should be done in the circumstances. The late doctor's remains were being kept, he discovered, behind locked doors until a decision could be made. We, of course, were already hours away towards the border. Once more, although we knew nothing about it, Chang-ch'ao took our part. In his truly generous and loving spirit, he had Doctor Bancroft's body removed and buried secretly. Oh Emily, I know that it must cause you great pain to think of any of this, but your late husband's remains were laid to rest with dignity and care. Think how he lies now in peace in a green grove that stands apart from the city in the very heart of the country he loved most — and take comfort from it.

Now I have saved the most exhilarating news of all until last, and I know it will put everything in its rightful place for you. When Chang-ch'ao told me, I remembered something that was said to you a year ago at Fan-ch'eng,

191

something that seemed to bother you, and I wondered at first if you had known all along. On reflection, I don't think so and I'm almost certain that what follows is new to you.

William, Emily dear, had no intention of leaving China. He had already told Chang-ch'ao as much the first time we met him back here, in Hsiang-ch'eng. He confided to him that he would be returning to the mission as soon as he had seen us safely embarked at the river.

Emily, I tell you this not to cause you more pain but because I am certain that it is your greatest source of comfort in your loss. William was coming back! He told Chang-ch'ao that a voice had spoken to him telling him to return for Chiang and Lin-sao. He said his heart was aching for them and for the Christians he left behind. Chang-ch'ao apparently tried to make him change his mind, said that the dangers were too great, but Doctor Bancroft said that it would have all blown over again by the time he was on his way back.

Oh Emily, how well I can imagine the feelings you must have as you read and as you tell all this to darling little James. Tell him I am going some day soon, when the weather is cooler, to make the journey to his father's grave; I shall put flowers there for him. One day he'll understand and he will feel so proud — the love, Emily, the courage!

I can't write any more. My heart is full with songs of praise.

In peace,
Martha C.

Emily looked out across the lawn, still shining from the rain, to where the elms on the other side of the river turned their leaves to the sun. Without looking down, she folded the letter again along the worn creases and slipped it back into the drawer of her desk.

"Martha and William," she said softly. "William and Martha."